PUFFIN BOOKS

Editor: Kaye Webb

DRAGON IN DANGER

It was nearly the end of Sue's second holiday in Cornwall, where her good friend R. Dragon had lived ever since the days of King Arthur.

The green dragon was very sad to think Sue was going so soon. She was the first human friend he had had for hundreds of years, and he was going to miss her. Then he had an idea – he would visit Sue in *her* home in St Aubyns.

But Sue was worried about it. How would he get there? It was certainly too far for him to fly. And where could he live? Not in her little house, for sure. Well, one way and another R. Dragon got over those difficulties, and he was soon nicely settled on an island in St Aubyns, and was even invited to take the star part in the local pageant. Everything, in fact, was going beautifully – until wicked Mr Bogg and Mr Snarkins began to plot against him.

R. Dragon must surely be the friendliest, funniest dragon in fiction, and if you want to know about Sue's other adventures with him, try reading the first book, *Green Smoke*, which is also published in Puffins.

For readers of seven and over.

Rosemary Manning

Dragon in Danger

ILLUSTRATED BY
Constance Marshall

PENGUIN BOOKS

Penguin Books Ltd, Harmondsworth, Middlesex, England
Penguin Books Inc., 7110 Ambassador Road, Baltimore, Maryland 21207, U.S.A.
Penguin Books Australia Ltd, Ringwood, Victoria, Australia

—

First published by Constable 1959
Published in Puffin Books 1971
Copyright © Rosemary Manning, 1959

—

Made and printed in Great Britain
by Hazell Watson & Viney Ltd
Aylesbury, Bucks
Set in Linotype Granjon

This book is also for
SUE

Contents

I

A Walk with a Dragon

FAR away in the west of England, as far as you can go towards the setting sun, lies the land of Cornwall. Its rocky cliffs jut out into the sea, and in its secret coves live mermaids, with ivory combs in their green hair, who ride upon sea horses with foaming manes. You would know at once when you reached Cornwall, because the roads are the narrowest you ever saw. They wind up and down between high hedges. Some of them are old dragon paths, down which a long, thin dragon could easily find its way, and some lead from castle to castle, and were the ancient roads of the knights who served King Arthur. All *they* needed was a path wide enough for a horse. They are not at all easy for large motor cars or caravans, or lorries, to drive along, and often you find cars stuck in the hedge, waiting for someone to help pull them out. Susan knew all about these paths because a dragon himself had told her. He was a green dragon, who had lived at the court of King Arthur, at Tintagel. He was rather shy and retiring, and now lived in a cave at Constantine Bay on the Cornish coast, and Susan had met him when she was on holiday there. She was the only human being he had made friends with for hundreds of years. His name was R. Dragon, but he kept the R. a secret. Susan knew what it stood for, but she would never tell anyone. You will see why, later in the book.

In was early in September when this story starts and Susan's second holiday in Cornwall was nearly over. Soon she would have to go back to St Aubyns, near London, where she lived. Susan was nine years old, and had no brothers or sisters, but she had three very good friends, Richard and Jeremy, who were brothers, and Natasha, so her sadness at leaving Cornwall was a little cheered by the thought of seeing them all again, when she got home.

Two days before they were due to leave Constantine Bay, Susan remembered that the dragon had promised to take her for one more trip on his back through the air, a thing she particularly enjoyed – and who wouldn't? – so she went down to the cave after tea and called out:

'Dragon! R. Dragon!'

There was a scuffling of stones in the cave and the green head of the dragon, with its shiny yellow horns, poked out from behind a rock.

'Good evening,' he said. 'How are you?'

'Just the same as I was this morning,' answered Susan, gaily. She had seen him earlier that day and had shared her elevenses bun with him.

'You can't be,' said the dragon. 'You are five hours older. People can change a lot in five hours.'

'I don't think I've changed,' said Sue, looking down at herself. 'I seem the same to me.'

The dragon stared very hard at her. Then he said:

'You look to me a *shade*, just a shade, taller.'

'Oh, Dragon!' cried Sue impatiently. 'Never mind my being taller. I expect it was all those sausages I ate for lunch. I want to go for a ride. You promised, you know. Through the air to Tintagel Castle. Do let's.'

'It all depends,' said the dragon, sitting down on the sand, comfortably. 'Is the wind in the right direction?'

He licked his paw and held it up in the air. If you do this, you will find that the wind makes one side of your finger cold, and then you will know that this is the side the wind is coming from.

'No,' said the dragon gloomily, gazing at his paw. 'It's *not* blowing in the right direction. I don't think I'd like to go flying this afternoon.'

'Oh, Dragon,' sighed Sue. 'You are a dear but you can be tiresome. I did so want to go. In two days we'll have gone home.'

'Gone home!' exclaimed the dragon. 'In two days?'

'I told you,' said Sue. 'I've told you *several* times.'

'What? that you're going in two days? I thought you said two *years*,' said the dragon, his large yellow eyes opening wide and gazing very sorrowfully into Susan's. 'Oh dear, this is a terrible shock to me. I don't want you to go yet. I shall be lonely. I shall miss you. Shall I speak to your father and mother about it? Persuade them to change their minds and stay here in Constantine Bay for a few years?'

'It's no good,' answered Susan. 'We have to go back. Daddy has to work and I have to go to school.'

'I shall have to think of something,' said the dragon, brushing away with a green paw what looked almost like a tear. 'Let's go for a walk. Walking helps me to have ideas.'

So, hand in paw, they walked along the sands, and neither of them spoke. Susan knew that the dragon was thinking and she had learned – as I hope you will learn – that when people are thinking it is very stupid to interrupt them. So, though bursting to speak, Susan kept absolutely silent. When they passed a starfish on the sand, she just looked at it and said nothing, and when she dropped out of her pocket a lucky white pebble, that she had picked up days and days ago and carried ever since, she never murmured, but left it sadly where it lay, while the dragon plodded on, with furrowed brow, still holding her hand in his paw, and saying not a word, but breathing rather noisily. Susan hoped that when the idea came it would be worth having. She was fairly certain that it would be. The dragon's ideas had always been good ones up till now.

When they reached Bobsand Cove, there was no one about. The dragon sat down on a rock.

'Are you listening?' he asked, staring very hard at Susan.

'Of course I am,' she answered, 'only there's nothing to listen to.'

'There will be,' said the dragon. 'Here's my idea.'

He blew a puff of green smoke from his nostrils, like a trumpet blast, and announced loudly and slowly:

'I – am – going – to – have – a – holiday.'

'Oh,' said Susan, rather disappointed. 'But you always do have a holiday, don't you? I mean, you don't work, or go to school or anything like that, and you live in a cave by the sea, all the year round. I call that having a holiday all the time.'

By the end of this speech Susan was quite indignant, thinking what a lovely life the dragon lived compared with herself. The dragon shook his head sorrowfully, and answered:

'If you always lived in a cave by the sea, it wouldn't seem like a holiday. I have to keep it clean, and cook my own meals, which is very hard work indeed. It's scrub, scrub, scrub from morning till night, clearing up the mess the trippers make with their paper bags, and ice-cream cartons. There's times,' the dragon went on, raising his voice, 'when I've worn my claws to the bone, picking up ice-cream cartons along the beach after a Bank Holiday. And there's times, too,' he added, fixing Susan with his eye, 'when I've hardly been able to crawl onto my sea-weed rug of a night-time, I've been so stiff and tired.'

'Goodness,' said Susan, appalled at this picture of an exhausted and overworked dragon. 'I'd no idea.'

'No,' observed the dragon. 'I didn't think you had.'

'Do please tell me more about your idea,' begged Susan. 'When are you going to have this – this holiday?'

'I'm thinking of leaving the day after tomorrow,' answered the dragon.

'Why not tomorrow?' asked Sue.

'Because the day after tomorrow is the day you are going back to your home in St Aubyns and I'm coming too.'

'Coming with me? To St Aubyns?' cried Susan, who could hardly believe her ears.

'Certainly,' answered the dragon, getting up, and starting to walk briskly along the beach.

'But where – where are you going to live?' Sue asked anxiously, running to catch up with him.

'In your house,' replied the dragon, calmly, and before Susan could say anything he went on: 'We'd better turn

13

back now. Your legs aren't as big as mine and I don't want you to get tired. In fact, we might go back by the lane. It's easier walking than the sands. Come on.'

So they turned inland, across the sand dunes, till they reached the narrow lane that ran along the back of the golf course to the village. It was one of those dragon paths I was telling you about, and as they walked along it, the dragon's head poked forward when they went round the corners leaving his back and tail out of sight.

'If you *do* come,' said Susan, 'and of course I'd love it if you did, dear Dragon –'

'I'm glad to hear it,' said the dragon, with a slight sniff. 'I was beginning to wonder if you really wanted me.'

'Oh, of course I do!' Susan gave the dragon's paw a squeeze. 'The only thing is, there really isn't room in our house for you. We'd have to find somewhere else. You wouldn't like a nice island, would you? There's a lake near us with several islands on it.'

'An island,' said the dragon, thoughtfully. 'It's an idea, certainly.'

'And there's another thing,' added Susan. 'How are you going to get to St Aubyns?'

'Is it far?' asked the dragon.

'It is, rather.'

'How far? Too far for me to walk?'

'Oh, a great deal too far for that. Several hundred miles. I suppose you could fly.'

'Not with all my luggage I couldn't,' said the dragon, firmly.

'Will you have much luggage?' asked Sue.

'My seaweed blankets,' answered the dragon. 'My pots and pans, and my washing things, and my scarf and my teeth.'

R. Dragon, as Susan had learned the year before, kept his teeth in a long box, like a pencil box, and only put them in when he wanted to look fierce.

'I haven't had to eat anyone for some time,' observed the dragon, 'but you never know, do you? There might be people in St Aubyns of such wickedness that it was my duty to eat them.'

'Oh, I don't think so,' said Susan hastily, thinking of all her friends. 'Only nice people live in St Aubyns.'

'Like you?' asked the dragon, looking earnestly at her with his golden eyes.

'Well, I suppose so,' said Susan, modestly. 'And like Natasha and Jeremy and Richard.'

'Are they friends of yours?'

'Yes.'

'All right. I promise I won't eat them, but I'm bringing my teeth with me, all the same.'

'Well, if you can't fly, I don't see how you're going to get there,' said Susan, looking very puzzled.

'You could take me in your car.'

'We couldn't possibly. You're far and away bigger than any car.'

'Not bigger than a lorry or a furniture van,' said the dragon slowly. 'Couldn't we hire one to take me up to St Aubyns?'

And at that moment, an extraordinary thing happened – just the sort of thing that does happen in Cornwall, and especially in old dragon paths and such magical places. They came round another corner of the lane, and there, stuck in the hedge, was a huge furniture removals van, with its back to them.

'Dragon,' whispered Sue, 'how did that get there?'

2

All England Furniture Removals Company Limited

Two men were leaning silently against the tilted side of the van, smoking. The dragon backed hastily out of sight, and hid his green and yellow head behind a large holly bush which was growing in the bank.

'Go on,' he hissed in Susan's ear. 'Go on and talk to them.'

'Your van's got stuck,' said Susan, by way of opening the conversation.

One of the men looked gloomily at her, and said nothing.

'Will someone come and pull you out?' went on Susan.

'Yus,' said the second one. 'Them piskies and fairies wot we hear so much about in Cornwall. We're just waiting for 'em.'

The first man stopped looking gloomy and smiled at Sue.

'Do you live in these parts, love?' he said.

'No,' she answered. 'I'm having a holiday.'

'And what's your name?'

'Susan. What's yours?'

'Fred,' he answered. 'And my mate, he's called William.'

Sue was rather stuck for what to ask next. She could not go on past the van, leaving the dragon behind, nor could she go back as the lane was far too narrow for the dragon to turn round in. After a great effort of thought, she said:

'Will you be staying here all night?'

'Till next Christmas, I shouldn't wonder,' said William, who had a long, sad face, like a dismal horse.

Suddenly a brilliant idea came to Susan, an idea which would solve all difficulties.

'I've got a friend here who could help you,' she said, rather breathlessly.

'Ho, yus?' queried William, in disbelieving tones.

'He *could* help you, I'm sure,' persisted Susan. 'Shall I ask him?'

'Go on,' said Fred. 'Be a sport, William. The kid wants to play.'

'I'm not feeling like playing,' retorted William.

'Well, I got kids of my own,' said the cheerful Fred. '*I'll* play. Where is he?' He turned to Susan with a good-natured smile.

'Just here in the lane,' answered Sue. 'You won't be frightened of him, will you? You see, he's a dragon.'

'Cor, me frightened?' cried Fred. 'It takes more than dragons to frighten me.'

'He hasn't any teeth now,' added Susan, comfortingly. 'He keeps them in a box.'

Fred laughed, and said: 'Come on, then. Let's meet this here dragon of yours.'

Sue held out her hand, feeling that Fred might need protection, and Fred took it, and let himself be led down the lane for a few yards.

'There he is,' said Susan.

Only the dragon's head and forepaws could be seen. The rest of him was round the next corner. Tired of waiting for her, he had gone to sleep. His eyes were tightly closed, and tiny puffs of green smoke were popping out of his nostrils every time he breathed. R. Dragon looked far more alarming when he was asleep, for you could not then see his friendly, toothless smile, or the cheering glow in his gleaming eyes. What Fred saw was a huge, green creature, with yellow horns between large cabbage-leaf ears, spiked fins down neck and back as far as could be seen, and heavy paws, all too well-furnished with claws. Fred stood and gazed at the dragon without saying a word. Then he turned back to the van.

'William,' he whispered hoarsely. 'It's true. She *has* got a dragon round the corner. I've just seen it.'

'Go on,' retorted William. 'It's the heat. You got a touch of the sun, Fred. Dragon my eye!'

'You go and look,' urged Fred.

'Not me,' said William.

'I'll go and wake him,' said Sue. 'I'm sure he could pull your van out of the hedge for you.'

Fred stared back along the lane down which Sue was hurrying to the dragon. Rather hesitatingly, he followed her. He turned the corner to see Susan shaking the dragon by a green, scaly shoulder, and crying:

'Dragon! R. Dragon!'

'Ururururururumph!' muttered the dragon, yawning, and opening one eye.

'Wake up!' shouted Sue. 'I want you to do something useful.'

18

'Too hot,' said the dragon and promptly closed his eye again. 'I can only be useful in cold weather.'

'Do come.'

'I'll ask you a riddle,' said the dragon, sleepily. 'Why are dragons and electric radiators alike?'

'I give up,' said Sue.

'Because they are both useful in cold weather. Ha! ha!' said the dragon, and scratched one ear. 'I think there's an ant hill on this bank. I feel tickly.'

All this time, Fred was standing, open-mouthed, in the lane.

'You see?' said Susan. 'He's a big, strong dragon and I'm sure he'd help if only I could wake him up. But he seems so sleepy. I suppose you couldn't go and sound your horn?'

As though in a dream, Fred walked back to the van and pressed the horn.

'Balmy,' said his mate, looking at him with a pitying smile.

The dragon heard the horn and opened both eyes with a start. 'What's that?' he asked.

'It's the furniture van,' answered Sue. '*You* know.'

'I don't know any vans,' retorted the dragon. 'Not to speak to, that is.'

'You saw it, only a few minutes ago, before you went to sleep,' said Sue, who had learned that you must be patient with dragons. 'It was stuck in the hedge.'

'So am I, ha! ha!' said the dragon. 'And very comfortable, too. I don't suppose that van wants to move any more than I do.'

'It does,' said Susan. 'And it wants you to help it. At least the men do. I'm sure if you pushed they could get the van out of the hedge.'

An idea seemed to strike the dragon.

'You did say it was a furniture van, didn't you?' he asked.

'Yes.'

'Aha! Then I think I will help it.'

The dragon stepped briskly forward on all four legs and went up the lane towards the lorry. His head and shoulders came into view of the vanmen. William went pale.

'Blimey!' he muttered. 'I've got sunstroke, too.'

'See?' hissed Fred. 'See? I wasn't making it up. There *is* a dragon.'

The two men stared at R. Dragon. William's face was chalky white, and his mouth hung open. The dragon was immensely pleased with the impression he was making.

'Aha!' he remarked, surveying the van. 'Got yourselves into quite a fix, haven't you? A nasty pickle. A – a fine kettle of fish.'

'Yes, sir,' whispered William, respectfully, touching his cap.

The dragon was delighted at this. He cleared his throat.

'It seems your van is stuck,' he said, adding kindly, 'in the hedge.'

'Yes, yer honour,' said William, touching his cap again.

'Calls me "yer honour" now,' whispered the dragon to Sue.

'Clever dragon,' whispered Sue.

The dragon, now in full view, advanced a few steps, folded his forelegs, and looked thoughtfully at the van.

'I could shift that,' he said, at last. 'I could push it up as far as the high road if you like, but in return you must do something for me.'

'Willingly, yer honour,' said William.

'What is it?' asked Fred. 'Want a ride in the van?'

'As a matter of fact,' said the dragon, coldly, 'that is exactly what I do want.'

He took Sue's hand and pointed with his other paw to the side of the van, on which was painted in large letters:

ALL ENGLAND FURNITURE REMOVALS CO. LTD
We take ANY thing ANY where
ANY time

'See that?' he asked. 'It couldn't be better.'

'What's all this about?' asked Fred, suspiciously.

'My friend, R. Dragon,' answered Sue, 'is thinking of coming to stay with me in St Aubyns. That's near London,' she added helpfully, thinking the vanmen might not be strong on geography. 'He is rather large to go by car, and we wondered whether you would be able to take him.'

'No fear,' said William, looking very alarmed. 'Van's full up.'

'No, it isn't!' cried the dragon, indignantly. 'I looked in just now.'

'Well, we aren't taking no dragons,' said William, nervously.

The dragon shrugged his shoulders and closed his eyes.

'Very well,' he said, after a short silence. 'Come along, Susan.'

'Wait a bit,' said Fred. 'Don't speak so hasty, William. We didn't ought to offend him.'

'That's better,' said the dragon.

'He's a wonderful creature. You'll never regret it,' urged Sue.

'You want this here noble animal taken up to St Aubyns you say?' asked Fred. 'How do you know we're going to St Aubyns?'

'It says you take anything, anywhere, any time,' pointed out Sue.

'Yes,' added the dragon quickly, 'and if you don't mean what you say, you shouldn't say it.'

'You know,' said Fred, looking at the dragon with admiration, 'I begin to like this idea.'

'Right,' said the dragon. 'Thank goodness that's settled. I'll get my things together this evening. What time will you come?'

'Eight o'clock,' said Fred. 'Where shall we find you?'

'At the bottom of the lane down to Constantine Bay,' said the dragon. 'I'll bring my stuff up there from the beach. You won't want to drive across the beach, I suppose.'

'No,' said William hastily. 'There are limits.'

'Now,' said the dragon, 'we'll get your old van moving.'

William climbed into the driver's cab and started the engine. Fred stood in the road and shouted directions while Sue climbed up on the bank to watch. The dragon placed his two forepaws against the back of the van and at the words

'READY! LET HER GO!' from Fred, William raced the engine, the wheels went round and round in a cloud of dust, and the dragon pushed and puffed from behind, his green face getting redder and redder with the effort.

Suddenly the van began to move, the wheels gripped the road, and with a last stupendous heave from the dragon, and a burst of green smoke from his nostrils, the van started off up the lane, making a great noise and dust.

Fred handed a red spotted handkerchief to the dragon.

'Would yer like to borrow it?' he asked.

The dragon mopped his heated brow, while Fred turned to Susan. 'He's a great fellow, your dragon friend,' he said, approvingly. 'Never met anyone like him.'

'I told you so,' said Susan, 'and I know you'll enjoy taking him in the van. He'll probably while away the journey by telling you stories. And now, please tell me when you'll arrive in St Aubyns because I'll have to find him somewhere to live.'

'It'll take two days,' said Fred.

The dragon handed a sodden handkerchief back to him. 'Thank you,' he said, graciously. 'I think we'll be off now. In fact –' he stopped suddenly, and eyeing Fred and William with a rather sly look, he added, 'in fact, Sue and I will FLY home. Come on, Susan, get on my back.'

Open-mouthed Fred watched Susan climb onto the dragon's scaly back, with its row of yellow fins.

'Now!' cried Susan. 'You listen. We just say a magic sentence, and you'll see us go.'

Fred sat down heavily on the grassy bank.

'Go on,' he said hoarsely. 'Let's see you. Seeing's believin'.'

'I'm for Constantine Bay,' bellowed the dragon, blowing out a great puff of green smoke.

'I'm for Constantine Bay!' shrieked Susan, waving her hand to the astonished Fred. The dragon spread his green wings and they soared up into the air and disappeared, for this was the magic they used when they wanted to fly anywhere.

Fred walked slowly up the lane to William.

'They've flown off,' he said.

'I suppose we're all right, ain't we?' asked William, gloomily. 'Not both of us going balmy?'

'We'll know tomorrow morning,' said Fred, and climbed into the van.

3

The Journey

THE next morning, Sue rushed into her mother's and
father's room very early, at about half past six.

'D'you mind if I go down to the beach?' she asked,
struggling into a jersey.

Her mother opened one eye sleepily.

'It seems a bit early,' she said. 'Must you?'

'Yes, I must,' cried Sue. 'R. Dragon is packing up and
leaving this morning and I want to see him off.'

'Leaving? Where's he going?' asked her mother, while
her father grunted and turned over.

'Wozzermarrer?' he asked.

'Sue's going down to the beach to see the dragon off,'
explained her mother.

'Off where?'

'To St Aubyns,' said Sue.

The bedclothes heaved like an earthquake and Sue's father sat up suddenly in bed, with his hair on end.

'To St Aubyns?' he shouted. 'That dragon's not going to stay with us, is he?'

'No,' said Sue, gaily. 'It's all right. I've thought all that out. He can make himself a home on one of the islands on the lake.'

Sue's father lay down again and closed his eyes.

'How's he getting there?' he asked, more calmly, as Sue ran to the door.

'In a furniture van.'

'Don't you want to make him a picnic lunch? He might be hungry,' said Sue's mother, who remembered the dragon's appetite, and how many elevenses buns she had given Sue for him in the past.

Sue paused.

'That's a good idea,' she said. 'I wish I'd thought of it. He can have my cornflakes.'

Sue rushed off at breakneck speed to the kitchen, seized a basket and put into it everything she could find to stave off the dragon's pangs of hunger on the long journey. There was half a loaf, the remains of a packet of cornflakes, some butter in greaseproof paper, three cold sausages, though Sue couldn't resist eating one, two bananas, a fruit tart, a lump of gorgonzola cheese, a packet of hard-baked water biscuits, which she hastily took out again when she remembered that the dragon didn't use his teeth, and, lastly, a bottle of orangeade which she filled up with water and stuffed in a corner of the basket.

'That ought to keep him from starving,' Sue said to herself, as she hurried down to the beach.

As she came round the corner at the bottom of the lane, she saw an enormous pile of boxes and parcels and oddments on the edge of the grass. Over the top of the cliff came the dragon's head, then his whole green body. He was carrying more bundles.

'My seaweed rugs,' he explained, panting, and flung them down.

'D'you really need to take all this luggage?' asked Sue.

'All this?' cried the dragon. 'There's twice as much as this still in the cave.'

'Goodness!' said Sue. 'I'd better come with you and see.'

They went down across the wet gleaming sands to the cave. Not a soul was about except the seagulls, and the sands were as smooth as a polished floor except where the dragon's feet had made long tracks across them. The floor of the cave was littered with his belongings.

'Where are all these things going?' asked Sue, in dismay.

'Into those two wooden boxes,' said the dragon, pointing to two enormous chests. 'Luckily, they were washed up on the sands a few days ago and I brought them in, thinking they might be useful.'

'But,' said Susan, looking at the scene with amazement, 'you can't possibly want all these things. What's this, for instance?'

She picked up from the floor a heavy wooden stick with a handle.

'It's a garden spade,' said the dragon. 'Or,' he added with a cough, 'a garden fork.'

'But where's the spade part?' exclaimed Sue. 'It's only the handle. You couldn't dig with it.'

'You could buy the spade part,' said the dragon, 'or the fork, of course.'

'But what *for*?'

'I might want to dig a garden on that island I'm going to live on. I might need to grow potatoes, or cauliflowers.'

'Nonsense,' said Sue briskly. 'And whatever's this. It looks like the lid of a sewing machine.'

'Oh, is that what it is?' cried the dragon in great excitement. 'The lid of a sewing machine! I *am* glad I kept it. How useful!'

'Why useful?' asked Sue. 'You silly old dragon. You can't sew anything with a lid.'

'I don't want to,' retorted the dragon. 'I hate sewing. I want the lid to cover up my food with.'

'Oh, dragon dear,' cried Sue, 'you *can't* take all this stuff. There's an old hair-brush, and *that* looks like a mangle, and here's a – a mouse-trap.'

'There might be mice on the island and beside it's very useful as a clothes peg when I do my washing,' said the dragon, hastily, and picked it up. 'And as for the mangle, of course I must have it, to mangle my handkerchiefs in.'

'No,' said Susan, firmly. 'You just can't. Look, I'll help you put all these things away and we'll only take what's really going to be useful. And we must hurry up. Time's getting on. I'll tell you a surprise, to make up for not taking all these things – I've got a basket for you, with provisions for the journey, like explorers have – there!'

'Susan,' said the dragon, solemnly, pausing in the act of picking up an old boot. 'Susan, you are a thoughtful and intelligent child. One day, you will make a wonderful wife to an explorer or a mountain-climber, and there will be pictures of you carrying a basket of food to the top of Mount Everest, or to the middle of some horrible jungle.'

After this, the dragon became more cheerful. He packed away his treasures more quickly, and, in the end, the only things he insisted on taking with him were a pink comb, a large piece of cork to use as a bath mat, the mouse-trap and the sewing machine lid. The rest of the things were stacked high upon the rock shelves, and the two big boxes were carried down to the far end of the cave. At last they went out onto the sands. The dragon paused and looked back at his cave.

'I suppose I am doing the right thing?' he asked doubtfully. 'I've always been very happy here, and I've got used to solitude and quiet.' He looked anxiously at Susan.

'You're going to love it,' she said. 'And anyway, even if you don't, you can always come back, can't you?'

'Of course I can,' said the dragon, with relief. 'Those are just the right words to say to an explorer in doubt.'

When they reached the end of the lane, the van was already there and Fred and William were putting the dragon's luggage into it.

'I suppose there's enough room for you,' said Fred.

The dragon peered in.

'What's all that furniture?' he asked. 'That isn't mine.'

'We don't go empty, you know,' said William. 'We brought a big load down to a house in Padstow, and we picked this up in Newquay to take back. By rights, we did ought to be quite full up, then we wouldn't 'ave no room for dragons, but it just so 'appens –'

'I don't know what you're complaining of,' interrupted the dragon. 'If you want to be full up, you will be, when I'm in the van.'

He started to climb in.

'Ah,' he said, with pleasure. 'There's a piano, I see. We didn't have them in King Arthur's time. It was trumpets and harps in those days. But a piano – I must see what sort of sound it makes.'

And he opened the lid and prodded a note with one claw.

'Very pleasing,' he said. 'Are you fond of music?'

'I likes a sing-song, and I can play a bit,' said William, unexpectedly.

'Can you?' said the dragon. 'Good. We'll sing each other songs on the way.'

He struck another note on the piano.

'Like this,' he said, and began to sing, in a high, reedy voice, to the tune of 'Old MacDougall had a Farm':

> *'Old R. Dragon had a ride*
> *In Fred and William's van–o!*
> *And on that ride he sang some songs,*
> *With a toot-toot here,*
> *And a honk-honk there,*
> *Here a toot, there a toot,*
> *Here and there a honk-honk!'*

'When you've finished, we got to get going,' said William, hastily.

The dragon leaned out of the van.

'Goodbye, Susan,' he said, and took her hand in his paw. 'See you the day after tomorrow.'

'Goodbye! Goodbye, dragon!' Susan cried, kissing him fondly. 'Have a good journey!'

'The basket!' cried the dragon, suddenly.

'Oh, wait a minute!' called Susan, as William started to shut the back of the van. 'It's his food for the journey. Where's the basket? Oh, here it is! How awful if it had got left behind.'

'What's in it?' asked the dragon, eagerly.

'You'll see,' cried Susan. 'Don't eat it all at once. Goodbye! Goodbye!'

And with a rumble of wheels, the van started to move away over the stony road. Through the crack in the doors

came a thin line of green smoke, which floated back towards
Susan in the shape of an X.

'It's a dragon's kiss,' she thought, and caught at it with
her hand, but it blew away over the cliffs towards the sea.

4

Arrival in St Aubyns

THE next day, Sue and her father and mother motored back to St Aubyns. They had just passed through the big city of Reading, when Sue saw what looked like a furniture van ahead of them.

'Oh, do pass it, Daddy, do get on quickly,' she urged. 'I'm sure it's the dragon's furniture van.'

Sue's father pressed his foot on the accelerator, and the car rushed along and soon caught up the van. As they passed it, Sue could see the letters:

ALL ENGLAND FURNITURE REMOVALS CO. LTD

'That's it!' she shouted. 'Make them stop.'

So Sue's father waved his hand and slowed down. The van stopped just behind them and Sue jumped out and ran back.

'Fred!' she called out. 'Fred! It's me!'

'Fred's in the back of the van with the dragon,' said William, for it was he who was driving. 'Having a rare old time they are,' he added. 'Playing chess.'

'Have you had to drive all the way?' asked Sue, who thought that the thin and sad-faced William looked more miserable than ever.

'Not *all* the way,' answered William. His brown face suddenly brightened and he whispered:

'Yon dragon's good at a sing-song, ain't he? We had a right good sing between Taunton and Newbury, him and me. All the old favourites – *Daisy, Daisy* and *Loch Lomond*, and the rest of 'em.'

'Did you?' said Sue, surprised that William could be so cheerful.

'Yes. Now it's Fred's turn. We take it in turns, see, to be in with 'im, so as he doesn't get lonely like.'

'How kind and thoughtful of you,' said Susan approvingly. 'Can I get in and see him now?'

But she didn't need to, for a green head was poking through into the driver's cab.

'What have we stopped for?' asked the dragon's voice. 'Have we got there? If so, I must comb my hair. Fred, have you got a comb? I lost mine inside the piano.'

'Here you are,' said Fred's voice, but William's interrupted:

'Look who's here!'

The dragon leaned out a little further and saw Susan.

'Goodness, it's Susan!' he cried. 'Hooray, hooray, hooray! Are we here?'

'Well, you're here,' said Susan, truthfully, 'but you're not in St Aubyns.'

'Here, but not there!' cried the dragon. 'Ha! ha! ha! I'm really rather glad because I don't want this journey to end yet. The only thing is' – he paused and an anxious look came into his eye. 'Excuse me whispering,' he said to William, leaning out past William's shoulder, 'I want to say something private to Susan.'

Sue stood on tiptoe, and the dragon stretched his long neck right through the driver's window, till he looked like a green giraffe, and whispered loudly in her ear:

'I've eaten all my food. Have you got any more? William and Fred kept offering me things but I don't like to take them. I think they need them, driving all this way. Anyway,' added the dragon, 'they're tough things, like cold mutton chops, and my teeth are packed. I can't get at them.'

The dragon looked anxious.

'You didn't hear anything I said?' he asked William.

'Not a word,' said William, staring into space.

'I'll see what I can find,' said Sue, hastily, and ran back to the car.

'Is there anything left from our picnic?' she asked. Her mother took the basket out and luckily there was – quite a lot – sandwiches, and two buns, and some lemonade and some rather soft bananas.

'They'll do fine,' cried Susan, and ran back to the van with them.

'Here you are, dragon,' she called, handing up the bag.

'William!' exclaimed the dragon, in tones of great surprise. 'I believe it's – yes, it is! Food! Sue's brought me some more to eat. That's very kind of your dear mother. Of course, I don't really need it (and here the dragon looked very hard at William) but I'll take it just in case. It might come in handy.'

He peered inside the bag.

'May I offer you a banana, William?' he asked.

'Thanks, mate,' said William, and took one.

'There *are* three more, I see,' said the dragon with relief. 'How much farther is it?'

'Not much,' said Susan. 'We'll be there before you. Will you drop the dragon at our house, please, no. 13 Fishpond Street? Then I'll take him to where he's going to live.'

'Come on, your move,' called Fred's voice impatiently, from the back.

The dragon leaned out towards Sue.

'That's Fred, wanting to get on with our game of chess,' he explained in a whisper. 'He can't play. I beat him every time, but he enjoys it. I'd better get back to the game. See you soon.'

He blew her a kiss and disappeared.

That evening, Susan and her mother had just finished unpacking the car when the furniture van came down the street. Susan rushed out and found that it was now Fred who was driving. From the back came the sound of two voices singing, one, the high one, was the dragon's and the other, a deep bass, was William's.

'Listen to 'em,' said Fred, grinning, and Susan listened. They were singing:

> *'It's a long way to Tipperary*
> *It's a long way to go*
> *It's a long way to Tipperary*
> *To the sweetest girl I know.'*

There was whispering and laughter and then the dragon's voice started again, with slightly different words:

> *'It's a long way to St Aubyns,*
> *It's a long way to go.*
> *It's a long way to St Aubyns,*
> *To the sweetest-little-girl-called-Susan that I know.*
> *Farewell, cave in Cornwall!*
> *Goodbye, Bobsand Bay!*
> *It's a long, long way to St Aubyns –*

Can't think of a last line, William,' said the dragon's voice.

There was a moment's pause, and then William sang:

'*But I'm on my way!*'

'But I'm on my way!' bellowed the dragon, after him, and suddenly there was dead silence. Susan then heard him say:

'William, we've stopped moving. We must be there.'

He put his head out.

'Hullo, Dragon!' called Susan.

'Why, hullo, hullo, hullo!' he said. 'I do believe we've got here at last.'

'That's our house,' said Sue.

'Where?' asked the dragon. 'I don't see any house.'

'There,' said Susan, pointing at her home, which was one of a row of little, old houses.

'Goodness!' said the dragon. 'It's so small I couldn't see it. How do you all get in? I can see I couldn't live there. I can't think how you turn round.'

'Well, I haven't got a tail,' said Susan, indignantly.

'That's nothing to be proud of,' retorted the dragon. 'Now, where's this island?'

'Could you drive down to the lake?' Sue asked Fred. 'It's not very far.'

'Up you get,' said Fred and Susan climbed up beside him and they drove off down the narrow streets till they got to the park, and there before them was a huge lake, and in it several large wooded islands. By now it was nearly supper time, and there were very few people about.

Fred drove along the edge of the water and no one saw the dragon get out. He stretched several times and his bones cracked like pistol shots.

'Stiff!' he exclaimed. 'Two days in a van is fun but cramping to the bones. I must massage my tail.'

He seized the tip of it and worked it vigorously up and down like a pump handle.

'That's better,' he said. 'Now my wings,' and he spread them out to full stretch.

Fred and William watched with admiration.

'Wouldn't mind having them wings meself,' said William.

The dragon looked warily round him.

'I don't want to collect a crowd,' he said. 'I'm not the Queen, or a film star – just a humble dragon.'

He coughed modestly, behind his paw.

'I'd rather have known you than any film star,' said William, gazing at the dragon with faithful, dog-like eyes.

'Thank you, William,' said the dragon. 'And now, if you'll hand out my things, I'll be popping over to my island while there's no one about.'

Silently, William and Fred handed out the dragon's parcels and bundles.

'I'm really sorry to say goodbye to you,' said the usually cheerful, fat Fred, wiping his eyes with his sleeve.

'It's been a pleasure to know you,' said the dragon, and held out his paw.

'We'll come and see you,' said Fred.

'Do,' said the dragon.

'The very next time we're in these parts,' added William.

'I'll look forward to it,' replied the dragon, and with a wave of the paw, he turned and picked up some of his bundles, and walked down to the edge of the lake. The van drove slowly away.

It took the dragon three journeys to carry his belongings over to the island on his back, swimming all the way. On the last journey there was an unfortunate accident. He was carrying his bundle of seaweed rugs, when, getting out of the lake, he stumbled over a stone, and dropped the bundle into the water. He pulled it out and sat down gloomily on the bank of the island.

'Are you all right, Dragon?' called Sue, anxiously, from the far side. It was getting dusky and she couldn't see him very clearly.

'No,' came the answer.

'What can I do?' shouted Susan.

'Fetch a doctor to tie up my toe, which I think is broken.'

'I – I'll try,' said Susan.

'No,' called the dragon, 'don't try. I'll bear it.'

'You're such a long way off,' called Susan. 'I wish I could see you properly.'

'I'll describe myself,' said the dragon, in hollow tones. 'I look very pale, and very miserable and very wet.'

'Oh, Dragon, dear Dragon, I do hope your toe isn't broken.'

'It's not only my toe,' said the dragon in a rather faint voice.

'Whatever else?'

'I'm feeling very upset. Here I am on a strange island. I don't know anyone. My friends have left me.'

'I haven't left you,' called Susan.

'William and Fred have,' replied the dragon. 'And now I have hurt myself and dropped my rugs in the water. I wish I'd never come,' he added bitterly.

'Dragon, I'm sure you'll like it better in the morning. I'll come and see you first thing, I promise, with your breakfast.'

'Breakfast?' The dragon's voice sounded a little stronger. 'That reminds me – I've got a little of that food left that you gave me this afternoon. Where is it? Where is it?'

'I do hope you haven't dropped *that* in the water,' said Sue anxiously.

'Here it is.' The dragon's voice sounded very much more cheerful. 'A whole paper bag full.'

'Oh, good,' said Susan. 'I think I ought to be going home now. Will you be all right, Dragon?'

'Quite all right,' came the answer, in a thick, crumby voice.

'Good night, then.'

'Good night, good night,' called the dragon, with his mouth full.

'Sleep well!' cried Susan.

A little cloud of green smoke floated over the lake and Susan was glad because she knew this meant the dragon had blown her a kiss and that he must be feeling better since he had found his food.

5

Pageant Plans

THE next day, Sue woke up to hear a great deal of noise going on. There were carts rumbling through the street and men arriving with lorries. They put up ladders and started hammering and banging.

'Whatever's going on?' she asked her father.

'Don't you remember?' he replied. 'It's the St Aubyns Pageant. It begins next Saturday. They're putting up flags and decorations.'

The pageant! In the excitement of getting the dragon back to St Aubyns, Sue had forgotten all about it. It was to be a tremendous affair, with hundreds of people dressed up to act the parts of famous men and women in the long history of the town, and a firework display in the evening.

Sue's friends, Jeremy and Richard, came hurrying round after breakfast. Richard was about a year older than Sue, and Jeremy, who was eight, a year younger. They were brothers and both had fair hair and dark eyebrows, but otherwise they were very different. Richard was practical and energetic, and wanted to be an explorer, or an underwater diver, but Jeremy liked reading and looking at things and just thinking.

'They haven't done much in your street,' said Richard scornfully. 'They've got wizard flags up in ours.'

'And banners and streamers,' added Jeremy. 'We've got one that says: "Come and see the Roman soldiers", and another with: "Famous fight of St Aubyn and the dragon". I bet that's going to be good.'

Sue stopped short in the middle of tying up her shoe-lace.

'The dragon!' she cried. 'I must go down and see the dragon at once.'

'It's not till Saturday, silly,' said Richard. 'Come on out and let's watch them putting up the grandstand in the field.'

'No,' said Susan. 'You don't understand. I must see the dragon. *My* dragon. He's a real one.'

Jeremy and Richard stared at her.

'What d'you mean?' they asked.

'He's real,' repeated Sue, patiently. 'I brought him back from Cornwall.'

Richard, being ten, felt himself rather above fairy tales, and laughed unkindly.

'It's probably some old lizard she's got in a box,' he said, but Jeremy turned directly to Sue and asked:

'Is he a *real* dragon? With wings?'

'Of course he's real,' said Susan, crossly, 'or I shouldn't have said so. And he's nothing like a lizard.'

'Let's see him then,' said Richard.

'He's on an island in the lake.'

'Oh, go on,' said Richard. 'You'll be telling us he breathes fire next.'

'He breathes green smoke,' said Sue, getting angry.

'I don't want to look at any crumby old lizards. Let's go and see the men putting up the grandstand,' said Richard, and he started to walk away, whistling.

'No,' said Jeremy obstinately. 'I want to see Sue's dragon. I'm going with *her*.'

They were outside the house now and Sue was holding Jeremy's hand. Richard hesitated.

'All right,' he said. 'I'll come to the lake with you, and we can go on to the field afterwards. Maybe the men will let us ride on top of the chairs on the lorries. That's what I'm hoping, anyway. Like we do on the hay in the summer.'

When they got down to the lake, they saw quite a number of people standing at the edge, pointing and talking excitedly, and clustering round two of the park attendants, who were looking hot and bothered.

'It's a disgrace! That's what it is!' one lady was saying, indignantly. She had a huge hat with artificial roses on it, and a very full shopping basket which she kept poking into the ribs of one of the attendants.

'An absolute disgrace!' she repeated, poking her basket, furiously. 'It's those dirty gipsies, I suppose. Allowed to camp out on one of our islands, indeed. Nasty, thieving brutes! You turn them off!'

The children looked across at the island. Hanging on the branches of the trees were several articles which Sue recognized at once. There was a green face flannel, and a woollen scarf, at least ten feet long, which was looped from branch to branch and seemed to go on forever. It was very gay, made in stripes of green and yellow, and had been knitted for the dragon by his dear friend, the mermaid, who also embroidered his handkerchiefs with R.D. in the corner. Hanging up as well were two browny-green seaweed rugs.

'If it's gipsies, ma'am,' a park attendant was saying, trying to hold the woman's basket away from his waistcoat, 'if it's gipsies, I'm sure I don't know how they got there.'

'It's not gipsies,' cried Sue, 'and if it were, I shouldn't care. I like gipsies.'

'So do I!' shouted Jeremy and Richard in chorus.

The lady in the flowered hat turned round on them at once.

'Ragamuffins!' she cried.

'We're not!' answered Sue, indignantly.

'They are probably the gipsies' children,' said the woman, pointing at Sue.

'She no spikka da English,' said Richard, rolling his eyes.

'There you are!' said the woman, triumphantly. 'I told you so. Ought to be locked up.'

And she gave one last bang and poke with her hard wicker basket and stalked away, with the artificial roses bobbing up and down on her hat.

'I don't see that gipsies do much harm,' said another woman slowly. 'They got to live same as we have. They've probably come to tell fortunes at the fair after the pageant. Good luck to 'em, I say.'

The park attendants were scratching their heads and looking worried.

'Give 'em a call,' suggested one.

'Right. AHOY THERE!' shouted the other.

There was not a sound from the island and not a sign of the dragon.

'HI!' shouted the first attendant.

'HOY!' shouted the other. 'WHO ARE YOU?'

There was a moment's silence and a tiny puff of green smoke rose above the trees on the island. Sue knew then that the dragon was safely there.

'Look, smoke!' cried someone in the crowd. 'They've lit a fire.'

'It was *green* smoke,' said Jeremy, slowly. 'I've never seen *green* smoke before. I wonder —'

'It's dragon's smoke,' cried Sue.

Jeremy looked at her with wide eyes. 'Is it a green dragon?' he asked.

'Yes,' answered Sue, but Richard still looked unbelieving.

'Couldn't it just be people having a picnic?' he asked the attendant in a man-to-man tone.

'It *is* a dragon,' said Sue, impatiently, stung by this treatment. 'He came up from Cornwall with me yesterday. Those are his rugs and his name's R. Dragon and that's why they've got R.D. on them, and he's green and breathes out green smoke and that was his smoke you saw just now.'

'Nonsense!' said a man who looked like a schoolmaster. 'Pure imagination.'

'Oh, let the little girl have her story,' said another, and picked Sue up and shook her playfully in a most disagreeable manner.

'You're all being very stupid,' Susan said crossly. 'And you're going to get a great surprise when you see him.'

By this time people were getting tired of the whole business and moving away. The park attendants looked at each other.

'Perhaps we'd better leave it for today,' said one.

'That's right,' said the other, with relief. 'Let's see whether the things are there tomorrow.'

And they, too, walked off.

'Well,' said Richard. 'Where's your dragon?'

'You'll see,' said Sue, but she wished the dragon would show himself.

'Everyone's gone,' said Jeremy. 'Do call him.'

'Dragon! R. Dragon!' called Sue across the water. But there was no reply, nor any sign of him.

Now, when Sue was on holiday in Cornwall, and first met

the dragon, she learned that he would hardly ever come out of his cave unless she sang him a dragon-charming song, and she used to find these charms written in funny old lettering on pieces of yellow parchmenty paper, under her pillow. The songs had to be sung to the tunes of nursery rhymes like one which began:

> '*Dragons are red, dilly, dilly,*
>   *Dragons are green,*'

and another which began:

> '*Dragon fairy,*
>   *Quite contrary,*
> *How does your green smoke blow?*'

Sue didn't like to sing any of them in front of Jeremy and Richard.

'I know the boys will think it's silly,' she thought 'but what can I sing? I don't know any new ones.'

She was a little tearful, and burrowed in her pocket for her hankie to give her nose a good blow, when she felt something crackly. It came out of her pocket with the handkerchief, and fell on the ground. Sue picked it up. It was a thick piece of yellowish paper. She knew at once that it was a dragon song. Carefully, she unfolded it.

> '*My dragon is over the water,*
>   *My dragon is over the lake,*'

she read, and in a flash the tune came to her. You must know it too. It is the tune of *My bonny lies over the ocean.*

'Look!' she cried. 'It's a dragon charm. I've got to sing it.'

She turned rather pink and while the two boys watched her in open-mouthed surprise, she stood on the edge of the lake and sang:

'*My dragon is over the water,*
   My dragon is over the lake,
My dragon is over the water,
   Oh come back, R. Dragon, come back.
Come back, come back, come back, dear dragon,
  to me, to me,
Come back, come back, oh, come back, dear
  dragon, to me.'

There was a slight rustling of leaves on the island but nothing more. Richard looked bored and disbelieving.

'Oh, come on, Jeremy,' he said. 'Let's get on to the field.'

'No, oh, no!' cried Susan. 'Do just help me first. You see, I'm sure he couldn't hear me properly. My voice is too small.'

'I can't sing,' said Richard, rather sulkily.

'I can,' said Jeremy. 'Oh, come on Richard. Don't be cross.'

'All right, let's look at the paper,' said Richard, rather unwillingly. So with Susan in the middle holding the yellow paper, the three children sang the dragon-charming song and it sounded very loud indeed floating across the lake.

There was a tremendous rustling from the island, several bursts of green smoke, and finally a colossal splash. The dragon was in the water swimming strongly, but he looked most extraordinary. His green head was covered with branches and twigs, and more branches were hooked over the fins on his back. Some of them fell off and floated away on the lake. Jeremy clutched Richard's hand.

'It *is* a real dragon,' he whispered.

'Don't be frightened,' said Sue calmly.

'I'm not,' said Richard, but Sue noticed that he took several steps back and turned very pale.

'Hullo!' called the dragon, in a genial voice. 'I enjoyed that song, with the three of you singing together.'

'He can talk!' shrieked Jeremy. 'How marvellous!'

And pulling his hand away from Richard, he ran fearlessly to the lakeside. Richard looked uncertainly at his brother. Then he swallowed bravely and stepped forward.

'Stay with me, Jeremy,' he said, and put his arm round his small brother's shoulder.

The dragon gave a beaming smile – he was very near the shore now – and said:

'I must get rid of all this twiggery.'

'What's it for?' asked Jeremy.

'It's camouflage.'

'What's that?'

'To make me look like trees, so that no one can see me. I could see you, though. All the time.'

And with that, the dragon rolled over and over in the water, and the branches fell off and floated away. The children were delighted.

'Oh, look at all the waves!' they cried, as great rollers came piling up on the edge.

'Are these your friends?' asked the dragon.

'Yes,' answered Sue. 'That's Richard and this is Jeremy.'

The dragon climbed out onto the bank and shook himself free of water, with a great shake that started at his green head and went all the way down his spine till it reached the very tip of his tail. He then held out a paw.

'Greetings,' he said politely.

Richard hesitated and then said 'Greetings', as well. Jeremy just gazed.

'Now,' said the dragon, 'we must decide where I am to go this morning. I should like to take a walk and look at the town.'

'All right,' said Sue. 'Let's work out a tour. A sight-seeing tour.'

'Like the man from Cook's!' cried Jeremy, who had been to France that summer. 'I'll be him. On our right we have the cathedral, ladies and gentlemen, and on our left the town hall. It'll be marvellous. Where shall we go first?'

'Well, there's the Roman remains,' suggested Richard.

The dragon shuddered.

'They sound horrible,' he said. 'Remains of what?'

'Oh, just remains,' said Richard vaguely. 'You know, pillars and things.'

'Oh,' said the dragon, without enthusiasm. 'They don't sound interesting to me. I never cared for the Romans anyway. What else have you got?'

'The cathedral,' said Jeremy. 'And the skating rink.'

'And the old market,' added Sue.

'And the fire station,' went on Richard.

'It'll do for a start,' said the dragon. 'Off we go!'

'Were those all your things hanging on the trees?' asked Jeremy, as they walked along the lake-side.

'Yes,' answered the dragon. 'I was drying them. Some of them had fallen in the water.'

Jeremy turned and looked back.

'You have your initials embroidered on your hankies like my father does. I wish I could have mine on my hankies.'

'What are yours?' asked the dragon, politely.

'J.C.R.P.,' said Jeremy.

'Too many,' said the dragon at once. 'Far too many. It would be all embroidery and no handkerchief. Very uncomfortable to blow the nose on.'

Jeremy was dying to be asked what his initials stood for, but the dragon didn't seem to want to know. So at last he said:

'Your initials are R.D. What does the R. stand for?'

'Oh, you mustn't ask him that,' said Sue, hastily.

'Whyever not?' retorted Jeremy. 'I like being asked what *my* initials stand for.'

'Oh,' said the dragon. 'And what *do* they stand for?'

'Jeremy Christopher Roderick Pagett,' answered Jeremy, proudly.

The dragon seemed unimpressed.

'I can't think what you want them all for,' he said. 'They are no use to you whatever. There's nothing you can do with any of them. Why have them? Now my name – which I do not intend to tell you – is quite another matter. It *is* some use.'

They had now reached the road, and as they went along, people grew quite excited and started pointing. In the general noise Jeremy whispered to Sue:

'I don't understand about the names. Why won't he tell us his?'

'Well,' answered Sue. 'If you tell a person your name – if you're a magic person, that is, like the dragon – then that person has power over you. If they call the name, then you *must* come.'

'Do you know it?'

'Yes, I do,' admitted Susan, 'but I promised never to use it except when I really needed him. If I was being eaten by a wolf, for instance.'

'I see,' said Jeremy, and fell silent in order to think this over.

So great was the excitement and hubbub caused by the dragon's tour through the town, that conversation after this became impossible, and they went on, like a triumphal procession, with the dragon and the children at the head, and a steadily increasing crowd behind them.

6

Wanted – A Dragon

Now while the three children were going on their tour of St Aubyns, the Mayor and several other ladies and gentlemen had met in the big field behind the cathedral where the pageant was to be held. There were to be two dress rehearsals that week, so that people could get used to their various costumes, some of which were very difficult to wear, being heavy with armour. The pageant was to open with the story of St Aubyn and the dragon. The man who was acting St Aubyn (he was really a local Bank Manager) had arrived, and dressed himself up in a long brown tunic with a girdle, and brown leather sandals on his feet. He was smoking a cigarette and talking to some men and women who were dressed up as early Britons. They all seemed very worried.

'It's Bert Robinson,' said one. 'He was told to hire the wretched costume, and now it seems he made some muddle in the date, and it's been hired to some other person.'

'Trust a policeman,' said another, for Bert Robinson was in fact a sergeant in the local police force.

'Well, we can't do the scene without a dragon, that's certain.'

'And we must have the costume to practise in — I mean, even if we made one ourselves, it'd be a good three or four days before it was ready.'

'It wouldn't look right, anyway. It'd look home-made. Fall to bits as likely as not.'

'What's the trouble?' asked an actor who had arrived late and was struggling into a tunic.

'Here, give us a hand,' he went on. 'I can't do this strap up, it's that stiff. What's the fuss? You're all looking very glum.'

'It's our dragon costume,' said a tall man, who had spoken earlier. 'Bert Robinson was told to order it and get it here last night so that Ted and I could rehearse in it this week, and he's ordered it for the wrong date. And it seems there's no other firm that does a big dragon costume like we want.'

The Mayor and two or three of those with him came over to the group of actors.

'Well, my friends,' he said. 'This is a bad business. We'll have to make a costume, I suppose. Make it out of sacks, or something of the sort.'

'It's disgraceful. Absolutely disgraceful,' cried a tall lady, with artificial roses on her hat. 'I really don't know what the police force is coming to. First they let gipsies camp on the islands, and do nothing about it (her voice rose to a shriek) ab–so–lute–ly nothing about it, and now that stupid Sergeant Robinson has let us down over the dragon costume, and my pageant — I mean, our pageant — will be ruined.'

Perhaps you recognize this lady. She was the one who had been at the lake earlier that morning, and had complained about the dragon's clothes and blankets hanging on the trees. Her name was Mrs Wotherspoon and she was one of the most important people in St Aubyns.

It was at this moment that the three children and the dragon came through the gate into the field. A crowd of people were following them, some a little nervously, others quite closely, overcome by curiosity. The dragon bowed graciously to right and left, as he entered the field, and the actors, who were waiting about, dressed up for the pageant rehearsal, fell back on either side.

'Coo, ain't he real?' cried a boy dressed up as an Elizabethan page, in ruff and feathered hat, and a suit of red.

The dragon blew a small, scornful puff of green smoke in his direction and went on. The smoke produced a sensation.

'Green smoke!' muttered one, and added, 'I say, he looks awfully real.'

The dragon could keep silence no longer.

'Of course I look real,' he growled indignantly. 'I am real.'

People backed away a little.

'It's real! It's real!' they cried, and: 'Where did it come from? Is it dangerous?'

'Of course he's not dangerous,' said Richard. 'We've been with him all the morning, and he hasn't eaten us yet.'

'No, but I could,' said the dragon, rather nastily, eyeing the crowd.

'But you wouldn't do anything so unkind, dear Dragon,' said Sue hastily, trying to be soothing. People backed away all the same, and it was then that through a gap in the crowd the Mayor and his party saw the dragon. All were

thunderstruck and stood rooted to the spot, except Mrs Wotherspoon, who advanced rapidly, the artificial roses waving wildly as she walked.

'A dragon!' she cried. 'Just what we wanted! Splendid! It's come in the nick of time.'

The dragon glared at her in great surprise.

'What nick of time?' he demanded.

'Oh, you can talk, can you?' exclaimed Mrs Wotherspoon. 'That's wonderful!'

'I can but I won't,' said the dragon, and shut his jaws firmly.

'That's all right,' said Mrs Wotherspoon. 'It isn't a speaking part. All you have to do is growl and rampage up and down and look very, very fierce.'

The dragon still said nothing. He closed his eyes and a look of patient suffering appeared in his face. Mrs Wotherspoon patted the dragon's scaly shoulder.

'You'll do this for us, dear, won't you?' she asked, coax-ingly, as if she were speaking to a small child. The dragon did not move, or even flutter an eyelid.

'You'll see, he'll do it,' she went on, turning to the crowd which had drawn close. 'He's a good dragon.'

At this, the dragon opened his eyes a little, reached for-ward and nipped an artificial rose out of Mrs Wotherspoon's hat.

'Now, my idea is this,' began the lady, but the dragon interrupted quickly:

'*My* idea is that we all join hands and sing "Here we go round the mulberry bush".'

Mrs Wotherspoon looked rather put out.

'That's not at all a good idea,' she exclaimed. 'No, as I was saying, my idea is that we quickly run through that scene with the dragon and show him what to do.'

The dragon reached out and nipped another rose out of Mrs Wotherspoon's hat. Some of the crowd giggled loudly and Mrs Wotherspoon glared.

'Where's St Aubyn?' she demanded. 'And the Britons? We shall need them all here at once, to rehearse.'

The dragon cleared his throat, and a little cloud of green smoke floated away over the heads of the crowd.

'Excuse me,' he said, 'but as I do not know in the least what you are talking about, I'll say good morning and be getting on. Come along, Susan, Richard and Jeremy.'

There was general dismay. The Mayor bent down and whispered in Sue's ear:

'I'm afraid Mrs Wotherspoon has offended your dragon, and we do need him very badly. Shall I have a word with him? It really would be a wonderful thing to have him in the pageant.'

'You could try,' said Sue doubtfully, 'but you see, he's

57

hundreds of years old and he doesn't like being treated like a little boy.'

'Of course not,' agreed the Mayor. He drew himself up, and in a loud voice, called out: 'Silence, everyone.'

The dragon took no notice.

'Come on, Susan,' he said, rather crossly. 'Let's go somewhere else. I'm tired of all these silly people.'

'A moment, Most Royal Dragon!' cried the Mayor.

The dragon paused and cocked his ears.

'Honourable Dragon,' went on the Mayor, 'will you deign to hear your humble servant for a moment?'

The dragon turned slowly towards him.

'I understand,' said the Mayor, 'that you are many hundreds of years old.'

'Quite a few centuries,' agreed the dragon.

'In that case, it should interest you to know that our town of St Aubyns is also many hundreds of years old, over a thousand, in fact.'

'Indeed?' said the dragon, inclining his head graciously. It was obvious that he liked the Mayor's speech.

'We were a flourishing town when the Romans came to Britain.'

'I remember their arrival well,' said the dragon. 'I was staying in Kent at the time they landed.'

'We were burnt by the Saxons,' went on the Mayor.

'Nasty fellows, those Saxons,' said the dragon. 'They killed King Arthur. Never mention the Saxons to me.'

'We rose again, however,' said the Mayor, hastily, 'and became a prosperous town. King Henry the Second made us a royal borough.'

'Most interesting,' said the dragon.

'Our first mayor was called Benjamin Wallop —'

'I knew some Wallops once,' interrupted the Dragon.

'Very nice people. They lived in a little hut in the New Forest and burnt charcoal, and knew the ancient magic arts. I had many a chat with them.'

'Probably relations of our first mayor,' said the present Mayor.

'I shouldn't wonder,' said the dragon. 'Now, Mr Mayor, I have been most interested in your little history of the town, but I think I ought to be –'

'One moment,' cried the Mayor. 'I haven't finished. I wanted to tell you that dragons have always played an important part in our town's history. Our patron saint, St Aubyn, fought a dragon – a bad dragon, of course, not like you – and killed him. A dragon appears on our town crest, and in the year 1463, a wicked robber was ravaging the town, murdering good, honest folk, and stealing their gold and silver, when one fine day in a dark lane very near here, he met with a strange beast who gobbled him up, and disappeared, leaving a note pinned up on a tree which said: "I, J. Dragon, did this, because I hate robbers." And the lane has been called Dragon's Lane ever since.'

The dragon grew very excited, and waved his green tail from side to side.

'J. Dragon!' he cried. 'Why, he was an old friend of mine! Goodness me, to think he once came here. He was a most useful dragon, always going round eating up robbers and wicked people. Well, well, J. Dragon! Fancy that!'

The Mayor mopped his perspiring brow with a large handkerchief.

'What a stroke of luck,' he whispered to Susan. 'Oh, what a stroke of luck.'

Then he bowed to the dragon and said:

'Most Noble Dragon, I have a boon to ask of you. Our historic town is having a pageant, as you see, in which will be enacted the scene of St Aubyn and the Dragon. Alas, we have no dragon. Is it possible – can we hope – would you do us the honour –?'

'I shall be charmed to act the part of the dragon,' said that creature, graciously.

'Oh, darling R. Dragon,' cried Sue. 'I knew you would.'

'Good old dragon,' cried Richard.

'Hurray for the dragon!' shouted Jeremy.

'Three cheers! Hip, hip, hooray!' cried the Mayor.

The dragon blushed pink with pleasure.

Just at this moment a little girl dressed up as a Briton came running out of the crowd.

'There's Natasha!' cried Sue. 'Hullo, Natasha!'

'Hullo!' cried the little girl, who was a friend of Susan's. 'I want to talk to the dragon.'

Mrs Wotherspoon, who had been keeping rather quiet and feeling rather small, at once caught her by the hand.

'No, dear,' she said firmly. 'The dragon likes to be left alone.'

'Oh, no, I don't,' said the dragon. 'I like little girls.'

He stared at Mrs Wotherspoon's hat. 'There's one more rose,' he whispered to Sue. 'Shall I eat it?'

'No,' said Sue, 'you mustn't. Please say how do you do to Natasha. She's my best friend.'

'How do you do,' said the dragon and held out his green paw.

Natasha shook it warmly.

'Are you going to be the dragon?' asked Natasha.

'I am the dragon,' he replied.

'Well, I mean in the pageant,' explained Natasha.

'That, I believe, is the idea,' answered the dragon. 'The Mayor seems anxious that I should oblige him and I wish to be agreeable.'

'I'm the little British girl that you nearly eat,' said Natasha.

'Goodness,' said the dragon. 'How very unpleasant. I have no wish to eat you at all.'

'You'll only have to pretend to,' said Natasha. 'Pretend now. Growl and grind your teeth. Go on.'

The dragon hesitated, then he turned to Sue.

'Susan,' he said in a loud whisper. 'D'you think I could tell your friend Natasha the secret about my teeth?'

'Yes,' answered Sue. 'I don't mind. She's my best friend.'

'Well,' said the dragon. 'Come where people can't overhear us.'

He and Natasha walked away and then the dragon bent over the little girl, and holding his paw over his mouth, whispered into her ear:

'I haven't any teeth.'

'No teeth!' exclaimed Natasha loudly, in her surprise.

'Sssh!' said the dragon, anxiously. 'I don't want all St Aubyns to know.'

'I thought all dragons had teeth,' said Natasha.

'Not me,' said the dragon.

'Have they fallen out?'

'Not exactly. I've got them safely, but I don't wear them now I don't eat people. I keep them safely in a long box and put them in when I need to bite something – or someone,' added the dragon, looking over his shoulder towards the Mayor and Mrs Wotherspoon.

'Well, you won't put them in on pageant day, will you?' said Natasha, gaily, for she was a little girl who found life amusing, and wasn't afraid of dragons, whether they had teeth or not.

'There's just one person I might need to put them in for,'

said the dragon, as they walked back to the others. 'That woman with the rose in her hat.'

'Mrs Wotherspoon? Oh, no,' said Natasha firmly. 'She's all right. Don't bite her. Besides, I'm sure she'd be awfully tough and stringy.'

'I believe you're right,' agreed the dragon.

Susan was extremely pleased to see how well her friend Natasha was getting on with R. Dragon. While they had been whispering about the teeth, the Mayor and his party had fixed a time for a rehearsal of the dragon's scene with St Aubyn at 2.30 that afternoon, and as it was getting on for one o'clock, the dragon suggested that they should all go and have lunch somewhere.

'What about up there for our picnic?' he said, pointing to the very end of the long field, where the ground rose up in a small hill with a clump of trees on the top of it. 'That looks very pleasant. Who's got the picnic basket?'

There was a moment's silence.

'Jeremy and I have got to be home for lunch,' said Richard.

'And so have I,' faltered Sue, feeling very uncomfortable.

'Oh?' said the dragon, eyeing the children in turn. 'And what about me?'

Sue began to realize that it wasn't going to be quite as easy as she'd thought, having the dragon in St Aubyns, if she'd got to provide food for him every day. It had been different in Cornwall, when all she had done was to give him buns for elevenses and occasional picnic teas.

'Well?' said the dragon, sitting down and folding his arms across his chest. 'Well? where's my lunch coming from? Am I expected to go round this pageant field, grubbing for half-empty ice-cream cartons, or WHAT?'

'Oh, dear,' said Susan in despair. 'I don't quite know,

dear Dragon. I'd forgotten you'd have to have meals when you came to St Aubyns.'

'How unfortunate,' said the dragon coldly.

'I did give you food for the journey,' said Sue.

'Maybe,' said the dragon. 'The journey's over now. I've eaten it all.'

'But you got food for yourself in Constantine Bay,' argued Sue, feeling that the dragon was being unreasonable.

'That was different,' he said. 'For one thing, there were fish in the sea, and crabs and such like delicacies on the beach. And then, there were farms where I could get (the dragon coughed and turned a little pink) – well, I could pick up odd turkeys and geese, that no one else wanted, you know, and always eggs of course, and milk. No difficulty at all. There isn't any sea here, as far as I know, and I haven't seen any fish in the lake worth speaking about, and there aren't any farms. This is a town, full of shops where you have to pay for things. I haven't any money. Dragons don't have money. And I'm getting hungry.'

There was a long silence. None of the children could think of anything to say. Then Natasha cried :

'I'm going to tell the Mayor. After all, if he's going to make the dragon act in the pageant, then he ought to provide his food.'

'Oh, what a good idea,' cried Sue, with relief. The boys said a hasty goodbye and went off home, leaving Natasha and Sue to find the Mayor. This gentleman, and Mrs Wotherspoon, were now right over by the gate, obviously on their way to their lunch. The pageant field was almost empty, except for a few people hanging round the entrance gate. The two children ran as fast as they could across the field, and caught up with the Mayor just as he was offering a lift in his car to Mrs Wotherspoon.

'Please, Mr Mayor,' cried Sue, 'we're in rather a trouble.'
The Mayor paused.

'It's the dragon's food,' explained Natasha.

'Can't he – er – eat grass?' suggested the Mayor, rather impatiently.

'Or leaves from the trees,' cried Mrs Wotherspoon, 'like a giraffe, you know.'

'He doesn't like that sort of food,' said Sue, and added, 'and he's hungry and getting cross.'

'Dear, dear,' said the Mayor, 'this is really rather tiresome.'

'Well,' said Natasha, 'you wanted him in the pageant. I think you ought to feed him.'

'I think little girls should be seen and not heard,' said Mrs Wotherspoon.

'You know,' said the Mayor, 'I'm not sure she's not right. After all, even a dragon must eat. Perhaps we could send something over to the field for him. What would he like, do you think?'

There was a sound of heavy breathing and a thin wisp of green smoke curled round their heads. R. Dragon had come across the field at top speed to see what was happening about his lunch.

'Ah,' he said, 'if you have a pencil and paper handy, I'll dictate my menu for today.'

The Mayor took out his pocket book, humbly, and awaited the dragon's orders.

'Now,' said the dragon, 'are you ready?'

'Ready,' said the Mayor.

'Well, I'll start with three grapefruit,' said the dragon, 'and sugar. I'll follow that with –'

'Roast chicken,' interrupted Sue.

'No,' said the dragon, hastily. 'I think not,' and he whispered in Susan's ear: 'Remember my teeth. It'll have to be something soft.'

'Chicken sandwiches,' suggested the resourceful Sue.

'All right,' answered the dragon. 'Chicken sandwiches, and tomatoes. About three pounds.'

The Mayor scribbled hastily in his pocket book.

'What would you like to end up with?' he asked.

'Banana splits,' said Sue, who had recently eaten one of these delicacies.

'Whose lunch is this?' asked the dragon. 'Mine or yours?'

'Yours, dragon, but you *would* like banana splits, I know,' said Susan. 'They're gorgeous.'

'All right,' said the dragon. 'They sound interesting. Several of them, please.'

So the Mayor wrote down: 'Six banana splits.'

'I'll get them sent over for you,' he said.

'You are a lucky dragon,' called Mrs Wotherspoon, from the car. 'Chicken sandwiches, and banana splits. My, I don't get lovely lunches like that.'

The dragon looked at her thoughtfully.

'Suppose you come and act the dragon in the pageant,' he said, 'and then perhaps the Mayor will give *you* chicken sandwiches and banana splits.'

Mrs Wotherspoon went off into peals of laughter.

'What a sense of humour he has, hasn't he?' she exclaimed, as the Mayor started the car.

The dragon scowled and muttered to Sue and Natasha:

'If that woman speaks to me again, I'll go back to the island and get my teeth.'

7

The Men from Potterfield

THAT afternoon, the first rehearsal of the dragon's scene with St Aubyn took place. The children were there, of course, only Natasha was not with them, for she was the little British girl whom the dragon was going to eat. R. Dragon soon grasped what he had to do, and succeeded in looking exactly as if he were eating her, when in fact, he was hardly touching her at all. He growled and blew out green smoke through his nostrils, and enjoyed himself enormously.

When it was over, the dragon and the children had a grand picnic tea, provided by Sue's mother, on the island in the lake. The dragon proudly showed them all his belongings – his sewing-machine lid, under which he carefully put the remains of the picnic ('to keep the flies off and the mice away,' as he explained); his mouse-trap hanging from a tree ('to pin up my handkerchiefs to dry'), his seaweed rugs, embroidered with R.D. in the corner.

'D'you know,' whispered Sue to Natasha, as the dragon was folding up the rugs again, 'd'you know, a mermaid embroidered the R.D. on his rugs and handkerchiefs – and I've met her!'

Natasha was very impressed with this.

'She lives in a house under the sea,' went on Sue, 'and R. Dragon has promised to take me to visit her there one day.'

'You are lucky,' sighed Natasha. 'I'd love to see a mermaid.'

'Never mind,' said Sue. 'You *are* acting with him in a pageant. I think you're lucky, too.'

At last, they had to go home, and they left the dragon spreading out his rugs and making his bed for the night.

Next morning, new posters, still damp from the printing press, were being stuck up on hoardings all over St Aubyns, and on the fences and trees along the roads leading to the town. The St Aubyns printers had been working till late into the night to get them finished, and very fine they looked, their huge black letters announcing that the St Aubyns Pageant was:

POSITIVELY THE GREATEST PAGEANT
EVER STAGED!!!
THE ONE AND ONLY PAGEANT WITH A
REAL LIVE DRAGON

The children stood in the lane on their way to the lake that morning, and read the poster with interest.

'They might have put that he was a *green* dragon,' said Jeremy.

'And that he can blow green smoke,' added Sue.

'I know,' cried Natasha. 'Let's add bits onto the posters. Who's got a pencil?'

'Pencil won't show, silly,' said Richard. 'What we want is black paint. Susan's home is nearest. Has your father got any paint, Sue?'

'I expect he has,' said Sue. 'Let's go and look, anyway.' So they went back up the narrow street and in at the garden gate.

'It'll be in the shed,' said Susan, and led the way.

There were several pots of paint but no black.

'Oh, look, here's a pot of green,' exclaimed Natasha, holding it up. 'That'll be even better. Come on, find a brush.'

Most of the brushes were old and stiff with paint, but at last they found a nice new one, still in its cellophane packet, so they took that one. Soon they were standing in front of one of the posters, and Richard was laboriously painting in green letters. He was frowning hard, and every now and again he stuck his tongue out with the effort he was making to keep the letters straight. The others watched him anxiously. When he had finished, the poster looked like this:

POSITIVELY THE GREATEST PAGEANT EVER
STAGED!!!
THE ONE AND ONLY PAGEANT WITH A
GREEN
REAL LIVE ∧ DRAGON
WHO CAN BLOW GREEN SMOKE THREW
HIS NOSE

'I don't believe that's how you spell *through*,' remarked Susan.

'Well, all right,' retorted Richard. 'How *do* you spell it?'

'I'm not sure,' answered Sue, 'but if you'll let me do the next poster I'll see.'

'I don't expect you can paint straight,' said Richard, holding out the paint-brush rather grudgingly.

'Well, I can try,' said Sue, 'and he's my dragon.'

They soon came to another poster, and Sue started to paint. It was far harder than she had thought and at first

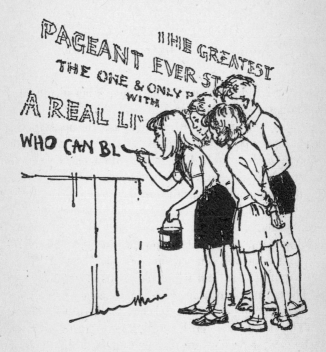

she used too much paint, and it started running down the poster in long trickles.

'You ought to have let me do it,' said Richard, in a superior voice.

"Oh, no, she oughtn't,' answered Natasha. 'We'll take it in turns. And Sue's doing it jolly well, anyway.'

So she was, only she didn't notice till after she'd finished

that she'd left out a letter in the word smoke, so that the
poster looked like this:

POSITIVELY THE GREATEST PAGEANT EVER
STAGED!!!
THE ONE AND ONLY PAGEANT WITH A
GREEN
REAL LIVE ∧ DRAGON
WHO CAN BLOW GREEN SMOK THOU
HIS NOSE

She had had a shot at spelling *through*, but it still didn't
look right, and Richard said so.

It was while they were arguing about the spelling, that
a car drew up and two men leaned out and looked at the
poster. One was fat and red-faced, with a very bristly, un-
shaven chin. He wore a black bowler hat, and a red woollen
muffler, although it was a warm day. The other was thin
and bony, with a pasty face, a glowing red nose, and sad,
watery eyes.

'What's all this about?' remarked the fat one. 'A live
dragon? It's a pack of lies, that's what it is.'

'Oh, no, it's not,' said Susan boldly. 'It's all true.'

The fat one looked at her very disagreeably.

'Dragons ain't real,' he said. 'They don't exist.'

'This one does,' retorted Susan. 'He's a friend of mine.'

By now, she was getting used to people who didn't believe
in R. Dragon.

The thin one turned to his fat bowler-hatted friend.

'It's nothing but pageant here and pageant there, all the
time,' he grumbled. 'Yer can't move a yard in this district
without you see some notice, or signboard, or placard or
something, to do with this blooming pageant. Fair sick of
it, I am.'

'Let's go back to Potterfield,' said the other, and then, noticing the pot of paint, which Richard had picked up, he said, ' 'Ere, wot yer doing with that paint, young man?'

'Adding some bits onto the poster,' said Richard. 'They'd left out the most important things.'

'Such as what?' asked the fat man scornfully.

'Well, that the dragon's green,' said Richard.

'And that he can blow green smoke through his nose,' added Sue.

The two men stared at the children.

'If you don't believe us, you can ask the Mayor,' went on Sue.

The two men looked at each other, and the fat one whispered in the thin one's ear. Then he said:

'If wot you say is true, young lady, you're onto a good thing, I shouldn't wonder. Wot about you showing us this dragon, as you says is your friend?'

Sue didn't care much for the appearance of the men, but she didn't want to seem unfriendly. She hesitated.

'Where is he?' asked the thin, red-nosed one, and smiled a rather greasy smile that was intended to be pleasing. ' 'Ere, would you like a sweet, little gel?' and he held out a grubby hand with a toffee in it.

'No, thank you,' answered Sue with dignity. And Richard, turning rather red, said:

'You can't bribe us like that. If you want to see the dragon, you'd better come to the pageant and pay for a ticket like everyone else.'

The others felt very proud of Richard for making this speech, but the men were annoyed.

'Pay good money to see a corny old pageant, and all about this dump of a town – not me,' said the skinny one, and his red nose glowed with fury.

'Nor me, neither,' said the fat one, and started the engine. 'Let's get back to Potterfield.'

Sue looked scornfully at the car and called out, as it started to move away:

'One day, you'll be sorry you missed seeing a real live dragon.'

Now, as a matter of fact, the men from Potterfield, which was the neighbouring town to St Aubyns, had every intention of seeing the dragon, even though they only half believed in his existence, and while the children were walking on, altering the posters in green paint, and spelling the word '*through*' differently every time, the men turned back into St Aubyns, drew up at a café, and went inside, where, over a cup of coffee and a cigarette, they had a serious talk.

'Now,' said Mr Bogg, the fat man, 'while I don't believe in such fairy-tales, it seems as though these pageant people 'ave got something, and if they've got something, why shouldn't we?'

'Sounds as if it's some queer, unusual animile,' said Mr Snarkins, the thin man.

'Queer, unusual animiles bring in good money,' said Mr Bogg. 'You can show 'em to crowds at a fair for sixpence a look.'

'We'd make our fortune,' said the thin one.

'But we got to get hold of it first,' said his friend.

The two men fell silent and stirred their spoons thoughtfully round in their coffee cups. Suddenly, Mr Bogg flung down his spoon, drank the last of his coffee, and rose heavily to his feet.

'Snarkins!' he cried. 'I got an idea! Why – don't – we – *kidnap* – it?'

8

A Food Fund for R. Dragon

THE following afternoon, another rehearsal took place, and though people were not really supposed to watch the rehearsals, the dragon was now so famous, that there was quite a crowd of spectators in the pageant field. Among the crowd, though the children did not see them, were Mr Snarkins and Mr Bogg. They lurked about, peering here and there, asking questions, and whispering occasionally to each other. When the dragon appeared, they grew very excited. But then, so did most of the others watching, and the behaviour of Mr Snarkins and Mr Bogg didn't attract any attention.

'Certainly looks like a real animile,' commented Mr Bogg.

'You can't believe it's made of painted canvas, can you?' said Mr Snarkins, loudly.

One of the bystanders looked scornfully at him.

'Of course it's real,' he said. 'This is the St Aubyns dragon, and very fine, too. Come all the way from Cornwall, he has, to perform for us.'

'Well, I never!' said Mr Bogg.

'You don't say!' exclaimed Mr Snarkins, and they nudged each other.

'He's a curiosity, and better than anything we've got in the Museum,' said another man. 'He's in all the evening papers.'

The speaker pulled a folded newspaper from his pocket and there, sure enough, were the headlines:

DRAGON VISITS ST AUBYNS

Another man took a paper from his pocket and there the two Potterfield men read:

NO COSTUME NEEDED FOR THE ST AUBYNS
DRAGON
HE'S THE REAL THING

'Ah,' said Mr Snarkins thoughtfully.

'Oh,' said Mr Bogg, and they nudged each other again.

The man put his newspaper back into his pocket and remarked:

'I left the wife making cakes and scones and I don't know what else. We've stuck a notice in the window saying: SEE THE DRAGON AND HAVE A CUP OF TEA. I reckon we'll get a crowd.'

'Really?' said Mr Snarkins.

'And they do say,' added a woman, 'that the Queen herself may come and see him. After all, he's a Queen's beast, as you might say, and no one's seen the like alive in England for I don't know how long.'

'The Queen herself!' exclaimed Mr Bogg. 'You don't say?'

'You're not from St Aubyns, then?' asked the man.

'No, Potterfield,' answered Mr Snarkins. 'The news hasn't reached there, yet.'

Soon after this, the two men slipped away, and if the crowd had not been watching the dragon going over his death scene with St Aubyn once more, they would have noticed the Potterfield men creeping off the field, their shoulders hunched and their hats well down over their faces. As they went out of the gate, their behaviour was even more extraordinary. They slapped each other on the back and uttered loud guffaws of laughter, while Mr Bogg even took off his bowler hat and tossed it in the air, whereupon Mr Snarkins neatly fielded it and handed it back to him.

No one saw them. At least, none of the crowd of grownups saw them. But one small boy did, and that was Jeremy. He watched them walk across the field and saw their antics at the gate. But he couldn't see the men's faces. He thought he had seen them before, but he didn't know who they were. Jeremy hadn't stayed with the others, because he was playing with Bing, the collie dog that belonged to the Bank Manager who was St Aubyn. Jeremy was trying to keep Bing away from his master on the stage. He would keep chasing across the field, and jumping at the actor in the middle of the rehearsal.

The dragon's scene with St Aubyn was at last over, and the dragon lay down on his back, exhausted. The children ran across the stage to him.

'Oh, Dragon, you were wonderful!' cried Sue. 'It was far more exciting even than yesterday.'

'D'you think so?' said the dragon, casting down his eyes, modestly. 'I've never acted before, of course.'

'It was super,' cried Richard. 'I really thought you were going to eat Natasha.'

75

'Ah,' said the dragon, suddenly sitting up. 'That reminds me. What about tea? It seems a long time since lunch.'

Sue looked worried. She hadn't liked to ask her mother for another picnic, yet how was she going to buy him things to eat? She had only sixpence a week pocket money. She'd brought out her shoulder bag, which had all her savings in it, but even that only came to half a crown and she knew it wouldn't go far. She saw that the dragon had his hungry look.

'There's a café place, over there,' he said, pointing with a green claw. 'I expect they'd be honoured to give me something to eat.'

'Richard,' said Sue, desperately, 'I want to whisper something to you.'

'Whispering,' said the dragon severely, 'is very bad manners.'

'I can't help it,' said Sue.

'If it's about me,' said the dragon, 'I'd rather hear it. Ah, yes, I see it all. You *don't* think I acted well, and you want to say so to Richard secretly, so that I shan't hear.'

The dragon looked extremely hurt. Sue rushed up to him and put her arms round his neck.

'I wouldn't do anything so horrid, dear Dragon,' she said. 'It's – it's just about your tea.'

'Oh,' said the dragon, cheering up at once. 'About my tea. That's different. What about it?'

And then Sue decided that it was always better to tell dragons the truth.

'It costs money,' she said, 'and we haven't got enough.'

The dragon stared at her.

'Susan,' he said, at last. 'I am the stupidest dragon in England. I forgot. I've foraged for myself so long and never paid for anything, that I never thought of it. Well, we must have a plan. Shall I – shall I beg like a dog? Will that make people give me food? I must have food, you know,' he ended, anxiously.

'You can have my money, while it lasts,' said Susan.

'And mine,' said Jeremy. 'I've got sixteen pence.'

'I haven't,' said Jeremy. 'I haven't got any at all. But I've got an idea. Why don't we ask the Mayor again?'

They looked round the field, and soon saw the Mayor and some other people talking together. They hurried over, and found Mrs Wotherspoon with him. She had bought some more artificial roses for her hat and the dragon eyed them hungrily.

'Did you want me, Most Royal and Noble Dragon?' asked the Mayor.

The dragon, after his acting success that afternoon, had decided to play another part. He put on a very fierce and hungry expression and growled:

'What I want is my tea. And I must say, if the people of St Aubyns can't feed their own dragon, after all I've done for them, blowing green smoke and bellowing and rolling about and play-acting, well, really, I'd better pack up and go straight home to Cornwall.'

There was a horrified silence. And then Mrs Wotherspoon cried:

'We need a special fund! The Dragon's Food Fund! I know, Mr Mayor. Give me your hat.'

In a trice, she had whipped off the Mayor's hat from his head and was hurrying round the field, hat in hand, begging for twopenny and fivepenny to feed the famous St Aubyns dragon. People gave willingly and it was not long before she had a hat full of money.

'There,' she said, triumphantly.

The dragon eyed the hat, and then, heaving a sigh, he said

'Madam, I am deeply grateful to you. You have saved a starving dragon. I am – er – glad to see that you have some new roses in your hat. Perhaps I ought to apologize for my behaviour the other day. I think I rather forgot myself. I believe I even *ate* a rose or two, but I expect I was hungry.'

'Don't mention it!' cried Mrs Wotherspoon, graciously.

Inspired by this generous reply, the dragon picked up her hand in his green paw and kissed it.

'*Noblesse oblige*,' he said.

'What does that mean?' asked Sue, who had once heard the dragon speak some Welsh, and thought this must be some more.

'It's French,' said the dragon.

'Oh dear,' sighed Susan. 'You can speak a lot of languages, Dragon. What does it mean?'

'Well – er – just *noblesse oblige*,' said the dragon.

'Yes, but – I still don't see,' said Sue.

'Well, it's just something you say when you kiss a lady's hand. I used to hear the knights say it sometimes,' said the dragon.

The Mayor came to the rescue.

'It simply means that they have made it up with each other,' he said.

So they all sat down in a very friendly fashion on the grass, and the children were despatched with some money to get cups of tea and plenty of buns from the stall in the field. Then the dragon kept them all enchanted with his conversation, as he told them tales of his youthful days at the court of King Arthur, and Mrs Wotherspoon ended up by plucking a rose from her hat and tucking it behind the dragon's ear.

'I shall call you Lady Wotherspoon,' said the dragon, and looked most gallant.

9

Mr Bogg and Mr Snarkins Again

AFTER tea was over, the dragon announced that he would
have a swim in the lake, and then retire to his island for an
early night. The children escorted him down to the lake,
carrying with them several bags of food which had been
bought out of the money in the Dragon's Food Fund. There
were tins of pineapple, and sardines, and potted ham, and
jars of marmalade, several boxes of biscuits, and a bottle of
lemon squash.

'That ought to last him for a day or two,' Mrs Wotherspoon had said.

As they walked down to the lake, it was only Jeremy who
noticed two men getting into a car and following slowly
behind them. He pointed them out to Richard, but Richard

was far too intent on listening to the dragon to take any notice of his younger brother.

'Oh, the tournaments were wonderful affairs,' the dragon was saying. 'Each knight had his own tent, with his colours flying from it, and as soon as he was called by the herald, he mounted his horse, and put his lance in rest, and at the sound of the trumpet he charged down the field against his enemy. As the spears met the steel armour, there was a fearful crash, which echoed round the lists. Sparks flew, and usually one of the knights was knocked off his horse, and lay like a beetle on his back, with his legs in the air. Don't you have tournaments today?'

'Only tennis tournaments,' said Richard, gloomily. 'With racquets and balls.'

'Doesn't anyone ever get knocked off his horse?'

'You don't play tennis on horseback,' explained Richard.

'No one ever banged flat, even?' asked the dragon.

'I don't think so.'

'It can't be very interesting, then,' and with this, the dragon dismissed the subject of tennis.

When they reached the lake, he rushed helter-skelter into the water, and splashed about a good deal, and blew out clouds of green smoke, which looked like green steam rising from a boiling bath. Then he collected up his bags of food from the bank, hooked them over the fins on his back and swam slowly and carefully back to his island. The children watched him climb out, take the bags one by one and put them in a safe, dry place, and then shake his scales free of water, like a dog shaking its coat. The scales clattered noisily, and Richard called out:

'You sound as if you are wearing armour.'

'So I am,' shouted the dragon, 'in a way.' And he stretched his wings and arched his back.

'Isn't he beautiful?' breathed Susan.

'Yes, he is,' agreed Jeremy. 'He's like a great green ship. I shall draw a picture of him.'

'So shall I,' said Susan. 'Show me yours tomorrow?'

'All right,' answered Jeremy. 'If you'll show me yours.'

As the children turned away to go home, two figures. one fat and one thin, could be seen walking along at the far end of the path.

'There are those two men again,' said Jeremy, and added suddenly, 'aren't they the ones who spoke to us when we were painting the posters?'

Sue and Richard looked over their shoulders.

'What does it matter if they are?' said Richard, carelessly. 'They only came to see the dragon swimming, I expect.'

'I don't like them,' persisted Jeremy.

'You don't know anything about them,' retorted Richard. But Sue took another look.

'They aren't awfully nice,' she commented, 'and if they *are* the same men, they were horrid about the dragon.'

'Well, it doesn't matter what they think,' said Richard, scornfully. 'They're stupid. Sensible people like the dragon. Even Mrs Wotherspoon likes him now.'

And that got the children talking about Mrs Wotherspoon and how the dragon had said *'Noblesse oblige'* to her, and long before they reached home they had forgotten about the Potterfield men.

As twilight came on, Mr Snarkins and Mr Bogg might have been observed, taking a small boat and rowing across to the island. The dragon was sitting with his back to a tree, gazing up into the sky, where the evening star, the bright star called Hesperus, was shining. It is always the first to appear and you can see it lying low over the horizon. The dragon liked looking at the stars. When Sue met him in Cornwall, the year before, he told her that he always bathed in a rock pool by starlight.

The dragon was surprised to hear the splash of oars and looked round to see who it could be. Mr Snarkins and Mr Bogg could not be seen very clearly in the dusk, and they put on such pleasant and polite voices that no one, not even a dragon, could have suspected what wicked characters they were.

'Good evening, Sir,' said Mr Bogg respectfully.

'Good evening,' said the dragon. 'Did you want me for anything?'

'Not at all,' answered Mr Bogg. 'We was just paying a respectful call on you.'

'Very nice of you,' said the dragon. 'I can't offer you anything, I am afraid, so I'll just say, "Good evening".'

'Good evening,' said the thin Mr Snarkins hastily, whereupon Mr Bogg gave him a push which rocked the boat.

'We don't want to disturb you, of course,' said Mr Bogg, 'but –'

'You do disturb me,' said the dragon at once, 'but I'll listen if you've anything important to say.'

'We – er – admired your acting,' began Mr Snarkins.

'Very much indeed,' added Mr Bogg.

'Oh, it was really wonderful,' went on Mr Snarkins. 'I'm a great one for the theayter and I've seen all the best actors. I can assure you I never saw such a performance as you put on this afternoon, Sir.'

'It was only a rehearsal,' said the dragon, but he sounded pleased.

'Only a rehearsal, of course,' said Mr Snarkins, 'but, oh, sir, what an actor you are! Believe me, I know one when I see one.'

'Very nice of you to say so,' said the dragon, puffing out a cloud of green smoke.

'You're fond of acting, eh?' suggested Mr Bogg.

'Well, no, I can't say I am,' answered the dragon. 'I'm doing this to oblige the Mayor.'

'Pity,' said Mr Snarkins, and shook his head sadly. So sad was his head-shaking that the boat rocked up and down a little.

'Why is it a pity?' asked the dragon.

'There's money in it,' said Mr Snarkins.

'I don't particularly want money,' said the dragon and leaning back, gazed at his evening star.

Mr Snarkins thought he had said the wrong thing, and started again.

'Wot I mean is,' he began, but Mr Bogg took over. 'You wouldn't care to do something for us, I suppose?'

'Not particularly,' said the dragon.

'Oh,' said Mr Bogg, rather dashed.

There was a short silence. It grew darker.

'Look here,' said Mr Bogg, at last. 'We been asked to put a sort of – a sort of extra bit onto the pageant. Right at the end. Actually, it's a secret. No one knows about it yet, but it's to be the smash hit of the whole show.'

'What is it?' asked the dragon.

'Absolutely the latest thing,' said Mr Snarkins, eagerly. 'It's a scene when a visitor appears from Mars.'

'How unlikely,' commented the dragon, without interest.

Mr Bogg and Mr Snarkins persevered.

'It's a wonderful scene. All the people of St Aubyns are there, when suddenly, a strange creature appears in the sky, and lands, and – it's a visitor from Mars! And you're the only one who could do it, Sir,' pleaded Mr Bogg. 'The only one.'

'Ah,' said Mr Snarkins. 'I can see you, sailing through the sky with them beautiful wings of yours outspread –'

'It's an idea,' interrupted the dragon, with more interest.

'I mean to say,' went on Mr Snarkins, 'it's all very well you fighting St Aubyn, but what happens? You just get killed. That's not right, you know. Not right at all. Just to let you lie there dead, and never see any more of you. After all, we don't see dragons that often.'

'You never saw one at all till you saw me,' said the dragon.

'That's what I mean,' said Mr Snarkins, at once.

The dragon was obviously getting interested, so Mr Bogg took up the tale, as Mr Snarkins had now run out of ideas.

'As my friend here has said, we've been asked to do an extra scene at the end of the pageant. Everyone's on the stage, see, it's the grand wind-up, when suddenly there's a shout – what's that? Everyone looks round about 'em, and then up into the sky, and people start pointing and waving their arms about.'

'People do too much of that already,' interrupted the dragon. 'Why encourage them?'

' 'Cos this time they've got something to wave about,' cried Mr Bogg. 'There's a thing in the sky, flying down towards the stage – something they've never seen the like of before.'

'But they have,' objected the dragon. 'They've seen me in Scene One and they'll all know who I am.'

'Not if you're disguised, as a visitor from Mars,' breathed Mr Bogg. 'Disguised beneath a layer of luminous paint.'

'Paint?' bellowed the dragon. 'You want to paint me?'

'It won't do you no harm,' pleaded Mr Bogg. 'It'll come off easy with turpentine, and you'll look wonderful.'

' 'Eavenly,' added Mr Snarkins.

'Like a beeyutiful dream,' went on Mr Bogg, 'and as you come sailing down through the sky, you'll say: "Ladies and gents, a very good day to you. I'm – from – *Mars*".'

So excited did Mr Bogg become at this point, that his bowler hat fell off, and floated away in the water, but he never even noticed it.

The dragon really rather liked this idea. It did seem to him a pity that in Scene One he died and was never heard of again. This would give him a chance to show the people of St Aubyns just what sort of dragon he was.

'Yes,' he said, at last. 'I like your idea. I'll do it.'

Mr Bogg and Mr Snarkins sighed deeply.

'What about a rehearsal?' asked the dragon.

'Now, that's just it,' said Mr Bogg. 'It's got to be a surprise. We don't want people to see you flying about, and practising. So what we suggest is this: you come over to Potterfield, and practise there.'

'I don't need to practise flying,' objected the dragon. 'I only need to practise my speech and a bit of magic. I can do that here.'

'Oh, no,' cried Mr Bogg, in agonized tones. 'Oh, no, that would never do. You got to practise landing, and so on.'

'Well, all right, I see your point,' said the dragon. 'I suppose I ought to practise a few antics in the air – rolling over two or three times, going into a spin, and so on.'

'That's it!' cried Mr Bogg enthusiastically.

'And you want me to do it at Potterfield? Where is Potterfield?'

'Oh, a few miles away from here.'

'And how do I get there?'

There was a moment's silence. Then Mr Snarkins said:

'Well, how did you get up to St Aubyns from Cornwall?'

'I came in a furniture van,' answered the dragon.

'That's the ticket!' cried Mr Bogg. 'We'll get a furniture van.'

'Perhaps you could get the one I came in,' suggested the dragon. 'I'd like to see William and Fred again. "All England Furniture Removals Company Limited", they were called.'

'Right!' said Mr Bogg. 'I'll get 'em if it's the last thing I do. Oh, this is going to be a wonderful end to the pageant!'

'Maybe,' said the dragon. 'I'm tired. Will you be going soon?'

'In half a minute,' said Mr Bogg. 'You won't say a word, will you? Not even to them friends of yours, them children?'

'Why not?'

'Well, it'd spoil it for them, wouldn't it? You wouldn't want to spoil the kiddies' fun, would you?'

'I'll think it over,' said the dragon, who was getting rather tired of Mr Snarkins and Mr Bogg. 'I'm making no promises. Good night!'

'Good night!' called Mr Bogg and Mr Snarkins, pushing off their boat.

'Don't count on me,' shouted the dragon, as they rowed away across the dark lake. 'I might have changed my mind by tomorrow.'

There was a splash, as Mr Bogg, appalled by the dragon's remark, dropped one of the oars into the water.

'This 'ere dragon'll be the death of me,' he groaned.

10

The Furniture Van Again

Two evenings later, the dragon was dozing in the early darkness, and dangling his long tail into the water to cool it, when he heard a shout.

'Hey!' came a voice.

The dragon decided to take no notice.

'Hi, there, Dragon!' came the voice again.

The dragon shut his eyes tightly and brushed a mosquito from his nose. He could hear a conversation going on in bass voices, and then the words: 'One, two, three!' and a tremendous shout came across the water. The dragon opened his eyes and sat up.

'Go away!' he called out firmly. 'I am either not here or asleep. In any case I don't reply to shouts. Go away!'

There was a pause and then a sad voice said:

'He doesn't remember us, Fred.'

The dragon listened more carefully.

'Go on,' said the other voice, more cheerfully. 'I bet he's foxing.'

'I am not foxing,' cried the dragon indignantly. 'I am dragoning.'

'I'm Fred,' shouted the voice.

'I'm William,' cried the other.

The dragon peered across the water, but it was too dark to see them.

'How do I know?' he demanded at last. 'You might be George and Dick, mightn't you?'

'But we aren't,' said William's despairing voice.

'In my young days,' said the dragon thoughtfully, 'it was the custom to summon a dragon with a dragon-charming song.'

Whispers and snatches of conversation floated across the water to the dragon's ears.

'Go on, William.'

'No, Fred, I really can't.'

'Yes, you can. Go on. You sang before, in the van.'

'Try *Daisy, Daisy*,' called out the dragon, helpfully.

There were more whispers, and then William's bass voice came over the lake to the tune of *Daisy, Daisy*.

> '*Dragon, dragon,*
> > *Give us an answer do,*
> *We're in St Aubyns,*
> > *All for the love of you.*'

The singing stopped suddenly, and the voice said:

'I can't get no further. If that won't do the trick, nothing will.'

The dragon opened his eyes wide suddenly, and they gleamed like torches across the water.

'There he is!' cried Fred.

'Coming!' called the dragon, and in a cloud of green smoke, he plunged into the water and swam to the other side.

The two vanmen greeted the dragon as an old friend. He was delighted to see them, and at once offered to show them his island home.

'It's quite snug,' he said. 'Now, Fred and William, you must come and see it all.'

'I'm afraid we can't do that,' answered William. 'We can't get over to your island without we have a boat, in the first place, and secondly, we got to get you over to Potterfield and move on ourselves. We're due in Glasgow tomorrow night. That's 400 miles, you know.'

'Ah, yes, Potterfield,' said the dragon, slowly. 'I'm supposed to be going there aren't I? D'you happen to know these men?'

'What men?'

'These men who want me to go to Potterfield.'

'Never heard of 'em before,' answered Fred. 'They rang us up and asked us to do the job, and said as how you was acting in some play for them.'

'All very secret,' added William.

'Oh, well,' said the dragon, 'I expect they are all right, only I didn't care for them much. They weren't – they weren't people like you two.'

'There's nothing special about us,' said William. 'We're just lorry drivers, we are.'

'Ah, but there is something special about you,' cried the dragon. 'One of you can play chess, and the other can sing. Very few people, in my experience, can do either properly. If you'd lived at the Court of King Arthur, you would have been held in the highest honour. Fred would probably have been the Royal Chess Player and William would have been the Minstrel William, who sang to the Knights after dinner, to the sound of his harp. I can see it all quite clearly.'

They went over to the lorry, and as the men opened the back doors, the dragon could hear William muttering to himself:

'Fancy me playing a 'arp! A 'arp of all things! Minstrel William, indeed!'

The dragon climbed in. It was a tight squeeze, for the van was rather full of furniture.

'This is like old times,' he cried gaily, as he wound his tail round the back of a large umbrella stand. 'Who's going to drive?'

There was a silence. Both men wanted to get in the back with the dragon, and they did not know how to decide which. At last, Fred said:

'Here, William, you go in the back with 'im, and sing us a song or two. Potterfield's only five or six miles off, and we shouldn't have time for a game of chess, anyway. Besides, you need cheering up more than I do.'

'That's real good of you, Fred,' said William, and his face brightened.

He climbed in, the doors were closed, and the van started to move away in the darkness. There was no one about. Not a soul had seen the dragon's departure.

While Fred was driving along the road to Potterfield, the dragon and William had time to sing a song or two, and Fred could just hear their voices over the rattle and creaking of the van. The dragon started off with his favourite *Daisy, Daisy, give me your answer, do!* but later there was an argument as to what they should sing next.

'*Shenandoah*,' suggested William.

'Don't know it,' objected the dragon. 'What about *Down in Demerara*?'

'No,' said William. 'I can't remember more than the chorus.'

'I'll sing the words. You join in the chorus,' commanded the dragon, and launched into *Demerara* at the top of his voice.

> '*There was a man who had a horselum,*
> *Had a horselum, had a horselum,*
> *Was a man who had a horselum,*
> *Down in Demerara.*

And here we sits like birds in the wilderness,
Birds in the wilderness, birds in the wilderness,
Here we sits like birds in the wilderness,
Down in Demerara.

Now that poor horse, he fell a-sickelum,
Fell a-sickelum, fell a-sickelum,
That poor horse, he fell a-sickelum,
Down in Demerara.'

Fred drew up at some traffic lights and turned to look back into the van. There he saw William and the dragon, side by side, singing the last verse.

'And here we sits and flaps our wingselum,
Flaps our wingselum, flaps our wingselum,
Here we sits and flaps our wingselum,
Down in Demerara.'

It was too cramped for the dragon to move his wings, but but he was flapping his front paws up and down, for this is the verse you must always act in time to the music, and William was doing the same with his hands. Fred doubled up with laughter, they looked so funny.

'If you could see yourselves,' he called. 'You look a proper treat, the pair of you.'

A loud honk from the car behind told Fred that the lights had changed, and he hastily drove on, still chuckling. William looked at the dragon.

'I didn't think you looked funny,' he said, solemnly. 'I can't think what Fred means. Did you think *I* looked funny?'

'Not at all,' said the dragon hastily. 'Oh, no, not at all. You looked very nice, William, flapping your wings, I mean

your hands up and down like that. Just like a bird in the wilderness. Ah, we must be here,' he added, for William was slowing up, and then the engine was switched off, the back of the van was opened, and there were Mr Snarkins and Mr Bogg. It was pitch dark outside. Not even a street lamp was in sight.

'Good evening,' said the dragon, politely.

Mr Bogg and Mr Snarkins looked a little surprised, but they said, 'Good evening,' rather grudgingly, and then turned to William.

'Better get a move on,' suggested Mr Bogg.

'No need to 'ang about,' added Mr Snarkins.

'No one is hanging about,' said the dragon, getting out of the van slowly and with dignity. 'There is no hurry.'

Unfortunately, his tail was still coiled round the umbrella stand and as he stepped out of the van, the stand fell on its side with a crash, toppled over towards the door and with a grinding of splintered wood, slowly slid onto the ground.

'Oh, dear,' said the dragon calmly, 'how very unfortunate. I hope it's not broken.'

'It don't matter,' said Mr Bogg hastily. 'We got to be getting on. Leave them to put it in. Come on.'

The dragon eyed Mr Bogg's dark tubby shape.

'Excuse me,' he said. 'I will come in a moment. First I am going to help William and Fred get this object back into the van. What is it by the way?'

'It's an umbrella stand,' said Fred, 'and it looks as if you've gorn and broken it.'

'Come on now,' said Mr Snarkins, and moved towards the dragon.

The dragon ignored him and started to heave the stand back into the van. He then stood still and brushed the dust off his paws.

'Ain't you NEVER coming?' groaned Mr Bogg and Mr Snarkins.

'Goodbye William, g'bye, Fred!' cried the dragon.

'Goodbye, goodbye!' answered William and Fred, shaking hands with him taking his scaly paws in their fists and working them up and down warmly.

'It's been real nice seeing you again,' said Fred.

Fred and William then climbed up into the driver's cab. Mr Bogg and Mr Snarkins were kicking their feet about and breathing heavily with impatience.

'Come on,' they kept saying. 'We got to get a move on.' They seemed very anxious about something.

The van engine started up and the big dark shape moved away. Its rear light disappeared round the corner and Mr Snarkins and Mr Bogg heaved a sigh of relief.

'At last!' they exclaimed.

'Where do we go?' asked the dragon. 'It seems very dark here. Don't you have any lights in Potterfield?'

'We're not in Potterfield, exactly,' said Mr Bogg.

'Oh,' said the dragon. 'Where are we, then?'

'Just outside,' explained Mr Snarkins. 'You remember. It's got to be kept secret.'

'Oh, well,' said the dragon. 'Tell me where to go.'

The two men came up on either side of him. Both were carrying a heavy stick, and looked rather as though they were expecting to have to deal with a dangerous animal.

'We'll lead you,' they said, and each with a hand firmly on his shoulder, they guided the dragon across a very muddy field, till they reached what seemed to be a large shed.

'In here with you,' ordered Mr Bogg, in a most disagreeable voice.

The dragon stopped dead.

'Now let us get this clear,' he said. 'I'm doing you a

favour. I've agreed to act a part for you. I'm not going to be ordered about. Ask nicely.'

Mr Bogg cleared his throat and said huskily:

'Please to step inside.'

'That's better,' said the dragon.

'It's no good annoying 'im,' whispered Mr Snarkins. 'Mind your manners, Bogg, or 'e won't do nothing for you.'

The shed was lofty and dark inside, and there seemed to be nothing in it but a pile of straw and a few dirty sacks.

'Is this where I am intended to stay the night?' asked the dragon.

'Yus,' said Mr Bogg.

'Then I don't think much of it,' said the dragon. 'What am I to sleep on, may I ask?'

'Them sacks and straw.'

'Oh, dear me, no,' said the dragon. 'I shall require blankets. Clean ones.'

'Can't get blankets now,' answered Mr Bogg. 'Come on, Snarkins, time we was going.'

The dragon began to move towards the door, but Mr Bogg and Mr Snarkins moved faster.

'Oh, no, yer don't!' they cried, and, rushing out, they slammed the great doors in the dragon's face, and put a heavy iron bar across them.

'Phew! That was a near thing, Snarkins,' exclaimed Mr Bogg.

They waited for a few minutes, but the dragon kept very quiet.

'Funny he doesn't growl or roar or anything,' said Mr Bogg.

'Perhaps he's fainted,' suggested Mr Snarkins.

Rather disappointed, the two men left the silent field. Inside the barn, the dragon, who had been holding his breath, let it out in a long puff of green smoke, and relaxed.

'Never get in a panic,' murmured the dragon to himself. 'Always keep quite calm in moments of peril.'

And with that he lay down on the cleanest bit of straw he could find, and thought very hard.

Early the next morning, the two men returned and walked across to the shed. Inside they could hear heavy breathing. The dragon was asleep. The Potterfield men had hardly slept at all. Their eyes were red-rimmed and their chins were black and bristly. All night they had been printing off posters on a small printing press, and they had driven up and down the roads around St Aubyns and Potterfield, tearing down the pageant notices and nailing up their own instead. Their poster, printed in heavy black letters on a yellow ground, read like this:

THE WONDER OF THE TWENTIETH CENTURY!

A VISITOR FROM MARS!

YOU'VE NEVER SEEN ANYTHING LIKE IT!

DON'T MISS THE MARS MARVEL!

ON SHOW IN POTTERFIELD

STARTING SATURDAY, SEPTEMBER 10TH.

Now Saturday, September 10th was the very day of the opening of the St Aubyns Pageant, and today was Friday.

Mr Bogg and Mr Snarkins stopped and hesitated at the doors of the barn.

'I don't know how we're ever going to get him into the cage,' muttered Mr Snarkins. 'I think he'll turn nasty.'

'We've got to keep him sweet,' answered Bogg. 'And food's the way to do it. We've got this bucketful for 'im. He'll be all right, you'll see. Arter all, he's only an animile.'

'Is he?' queried Mr Snarkins. 'I'm not so sure. He can talk. I think you got to treat him differently.'

'I think you got to treat him rough,' said Mr Bogg firmly. 'You leave this to me.'

He banged loudly on the door and said, ' 'Ere we are!'

The two men lifted the great bar, and went into the barn.

The dragon opened one eye.

'What a way to come in,' he said and scowled. ' 'Ere we are, indeed! I wonder what King Arthur would have said to his knights, if they had entered the castle hall and said, " 'Ere we are!" '

This rather dumbfounded Mr Bogg and Mr Snarkins.

'Well, 'ere we are, anyway,' said Mr Snarkins feebly.

'So you said before,' remarked the dragon, giving a yawn. 'If you'll put down that bucket, I'll teach you how to enter properly.'

Obediently, Mr Snarkins put down the bucket. The dragon sat up, and brushed the straw from his ears.

'Entering my hall,' he said, 'you should bow low and say: "Most Noble Dragon, at your service." '

'Now look 'ere,' began Mr Bogg angrily, but Mr Snarkins poked him in the ribs.

'You pipe down,' he whispered. 'We got to humour him.' And he walked over to the door.

'Like this?' he queried, and giving a rather clumsy bow, he said: 'Most Noble Dragon, at yer service, yer humble servants, Bogg and Snarkins.'

The dragon smiled graciously.

'Good morning to you,' he said. 'And what can I do for you, Mr – er – Snogg and Mr Barkins.'

'You ain't forgotten, you're acting the part of a visitor from Mars?'

'No, I remember,' said the dragon. 'Let's get the rehearsing over. I want to get back to St Aubyns.'

'Have yer breakfast first,' suggested Mr Bogg, and put the bucket down in front of the dragon, who took one look at it, and then lifted his nose in the air and walked in dignified silence towards the open door.

' 'E's getting away,' said Bogg, in a husky whisper. 'Quick, stop 'im!'

Both men rushed to the door, but the dragon was out before them. He snuffed the fresh air, and then, looking round him, said:

'If by breakfast you mean that bucket of pig-wash, think again.'

'If there's anything else you fancy –' began Mr Snarkins.

'Yes, there is, Mr Barkins,' interrupted the dragon. 'Apart from sixteen boiled eggs, nine toasted crumpets and a two pound pot of marmalade, I would like the following: I would like to know what you and Mr Snoggs here are up to, because I think you're up to no good.'

Mr Snarkins looked despairingly at Mr Bogg.

'He's seen it all,' he whispered. But Mr Bogg was made of sterner stuff. He was not one to give up easily.

'You go back into that shed,' he said firmly to the dragon, 'and we'll explain.'

The dragon did not move.

'No,' he said. 'You go first.'

'Go on, Snarkins,' ordered Mr Bogg, and whispered quickly in his friend's ear.

Mr Snarkins went inside the barn and called out:

'We wasn't sure you'd like what was in the bucket, Sir, so we brought something else.'

'What?' asked the dragon.

'Well, there's a pound bar of chocolate,' suggested Mr Snarkins, in a soft, alluring voice. 'And – lemme see – there's a couple of rock cakes what my wife made, and – er – a packet of digestive biscuits.'

Now the dragon really was, by this time, extremely hungry. Moreover, as you know, he was very, very fond of his food, and Mr Snarkins' list made his mouth water.

'Have you really got all that?' he asked, uncertainly.

Mr Snarkins, of course, had not got any of it, but he pulled a piece of paper out of his pocket and made a crackly sound with it.

'I'm just unwrapping the chocolate,' he said.

It was too much for the dragon. Trying not to look too eager, he hurried into the barn. And so it was that Mr Snarkins and the dragon were shut in together, for no sooner had Mr Bogg seen them both safely inside, than he wickedly slammed the door and barred it.

For a moment there was silence. Then Mr Snarkins's voice came to the ears of the traitor, Bogg.

'Please, Sir, don't eat me! I didn't mean no harm. Oh, Most Noble Dragon, please, please, don't eat me!'

'Ha, ha!' laughed the unpleasant Mr Bogg outside the door.

Now, as a matter of fact, the dragon couldn't eat Mr Snarkins, much as he would have liked to, because, as you will remember, he had no teeth. But Mr Bogg did not know this.

'Let me out!' cried Mr Snarkins. 'Henery Bogg, never did I think this of you. Let me out!'

'No, I won't,' shouted Mr Bogg. 'You been too soft with that dragon, and now look what's happened to you. No, you can stay there till Saturday, and – and if you're hungry, you can eat each other!'

With which unkind remark, Mr Bogg walked away.

II

A Very Black Friday

MEANWHILE, in St Aubyns, the children had been puzzled at the dragon's absence. They had gone down to the lake after breakfast, carrying food for him in a large brown paper carrier, labelled Morgan & Son, High Class Fruiterers. But their calls brought no reply and neither did a joint singing effort of *My dragon is over the water*.

'Perhaps he is ill,' said Sue anxiously. 'Couldn't we go and look?'

After a slight argument, the boat-house man agreed to let them have a boat, but sent his boy with them to row it, which annoyed Richard very much. He had been hoping to show off to the others his skill as an oarsman, so he sulked in the stern of the boat, while Jeremy was allowed by the boat-man's boy to take one of the oars, and enjoyed himself very much. The two girls were far too anxious about the dragon to bother with either Richard or Jeremy. They sat in the bow of the boat holding hands and peering out towards the island. The boat-man's boy moored the skiff to a tree and said:

'You can land on the island and have a look round, if you like, but be sharp about it. I haven't got all the morning to spare.'

The children jumped ashore. It didn't take long to search the island for it was only a small one. There was the dragon's bed, which he had made of dried grass, with his seaweed blankets spread over it. There was his mouse-trap hung on a tree, a green handkerchief with R.D. embroidered in the corner, fluttering from it. There was his sewing machine lid. She could have cried. She clutched Natasha's hand.

'What can have happened to him?' she said. 'Supposing he went for a walk or something, or a swim, and got hurt?'

'Don't,' said Natasha. 'It's too awful to think of.'

'I don't believe he's hurt,' said Richard, as the boy rowed them back. 'I just think he's got bored, and gone for a walk. He'll turn up for lunch, you'll see.'

But R. Dragon did not turn up for lunch, nor for tea, and when the children, after searching all day long, went home tired and out of sorts at the end of it, R. Dragon was still missing.

While the Mayor and all St Aubyns had joined in the search, Mr Bogg had been very busy indeed. He had already hired a large field from a local farmer, and on that dreadful Friday, he spent most of his time down there, looking on and getting in the way, while a firm of builders put up a wooden ticket office at the gate. He also had to interview a steady stream of people with ice-cream carts and sweet barrows and coconut stalls and fortune-telling tents, who had all heard of Potterfield's Visitor from Mars, and wanted to set up their stalls and barrows in the same field, to make some money out of the crowds who would come to see the Mars man. Mr Bogg was very pleased.

'The more the merrier!' he cried, as the barrows rolled up. 'It'll be like a fair! The more the merrier!'

Many people asked him where the Visitor from Mars was, but this Mr Bogg refused to say.

At last, about four o'clock, the field was ready. Mr Bogg was very tired and hungry, for he had had no time to eat any lunch. But he felt pleased with his day's work. The field looked very festive and gay. Bunting hung from the stalls, and a huge banner, fixed to poles, was at the entrance gates, reading:

THE VISITOR FROM MARS WELCOMES YOU!

A couple of men were installed in the ticket office, ready to deal with the crowds. Mr Bogg was delighted that Mr Snarkins was no longer with him.

'Aha!' he said to himself, as he peered into the ticket office and saw the rolls of tickets at one shilling each. 'Aha! All that will be for me! I shan't have to share it with Snarkins now.'

This reminded him that the dragon and Mr Snarkins were still shut up in the shed and might well need some food, if they had not already eaten each other.

'I'll have to take some down to them,' he said to himself. 'But I'll have some myself, first.'

So Mr Bogg went home and had a huge high tea. He ate six rashers of bacon and three eggs, at least half a loaf of bread and butter, thickly cut, and two slices of Dundee cake. He washed all this down with several cups of very strong, sweet tea. Then he sat back and thought about how he was going to get the dragon from the shed to the show field, which was about half a mile away. He had hired from a circus one of the big travelling cages used for lions and tigers, and this had already arrived and was waiting near the shed. The question was, how to persuade the dragon to get into it. He had discussed this with Mr Snarkins when they had first plotted the whole scheme of kidnapping the dragon.

'How are we going to get him into the cage?' Mr Snarkins had asked.

'Knock 'im on the head,' Mr Bogg had suggested. 'Stun 'im.'

But Mr Snarkins had objected.

'In the first place,' he had said, 'you might really hurt him, and in the second, if he turned nasty you couldn't get near him to knock him on the head, and what's more he wouldn't act for you. No, what you got to do, Bogg, is to put a sleeping pill into his food, one of the sort that will make him easy to handle.'

Remembering this, Mr Bogg, whose heart was black with wickedness, thought it a very good idea, and felt quite grateful to Mr Snarkins. He pushed away his plate, got up and placed his new bowler hat upon his head. He took a large leather shopping bag from the kitchen, and called out to his wife, who was in the back garden:

'Shan't be back for an hour, Em. Don't forget to feed the cat.'

Which shows that Mr Bogg was not entirely bad. Where his cat was concerned, he could be thoughtful.

Mr Bogg went first to a chemist's shop to buy the special sleeping pills, and then to a grocer's. When he had finished shopping, his leather bag was overflowing. He took a bus to the outskirts of Potterfield and then walked along the quiet, muddy lane to the field where the shed was. Inside the shed, Mr Bogg could hear voices. He put his ear to the wooden wall and listened.

'And then,' the dragon's voice said, 'King Arthur cried: "Noble Dragon! You have done me good and faithful service. With my sword I dub thee knight." And with that he struck me lightly on the shoulder with the blade of his sword, and said: "Arise, Sir Dragon!"'

'And you're really *Sir* Dragon?' came the astonished and awestruck voice of Mr Snarkins.

'Well, yes.' The dragon sounded rather sad. 'I don't use the title, of course, now. The Knights of the Round Table are no more, and King Arthur has departed, so there seems no point.'

'I'll always call you Sir Dragon, if you like,' said Mr Snarkins.

'It's kind of you,' said the dragon, giving a sniff, 'but it wouldn't be quite the same thing.'

'King Arthur?' muttered Mr Bogg. 'Round Table? Sir Dragon? It don't make sense to me. They've gone balmy, the pair of them.'

Mr Bogg now rapped loudly on the shed door with his stick and called out:

'You two eaten each other yet?'

There was a moment's silence and then the dragon said:

'Not yet, though I'm getting hungry,' and he growled fiercely.

'Oh, don't, Sir, please don't!' came Mr Snarkins' voice, but it sounded rather as though he were trying not to laugh.

'I've brought you some food,' said Mr Bogg.

'Very kind of you,' said the dragon. 'Do come in.'

'Ho, no!' said Mr Bogg. 'I'm not going to be caught that way.'

'Well, in that case,' suggested the dragon, 'perhaps we'll come out.'

'No, yer don't,' said Mr Bogg, hastily. 'There's a rat hole near this 'ere door, and I'm going to put the food 'ere, see? and you can reach for it.'

'Very well,' said the dragon. 'Only mind my claws. They're sharp.'

Mr Bogg thought he could hear a suppressed giggle from Mr Snarkins, but he couldn't be certain. He held the bag to the hole and out came a green, scaly paw, with very long claws. Mr Bogg backed away a little and then pushed the bag forward with the end of his walking-stick. The dragon's paw gripped the stick as well as the bag and drew both into the barn.

'Hi!' cried Mr Bogg. 'My walking-stick!'

'Come in and get it,' said the dragon, and laughed.

Mr Bogg hesitated.

'No, I won't,' he said at last, through the hole. 'You can give it to Snarkins with my compliments.'

'I have already,' replied the dragon. 'He's walking up and down with it now. He likes it very much. He says he's always wanted a walking-stick with a parrot's-head handle.'

Mr Bogg snorted with annoyance. Then, suddenly remembering something important, he called:

'The sausage rolls are specially good. Eat them first.'

With that, he made sure that the bar was still securely fastened across the shed door and went home. On the way, he bought an evening paper. The headlines were particularly pleasing to the wicked Mr Bogg.

DRAGON VANISHES FROM ST AUBYNS!
POLICE CALLED IN

Underneath this, Mr Bogg read:

Some people are asking: Was there ever a dragon at St Aubyns at all? Was the whole thing a trick? Whatever it was, the dragon is not there now, and tomorrow, when the St Aubyns Pageant opens, it will be without its dragon. We understand that the first scene, which showed the historic fight between St Aubyn and the dragon, has had to be cut.

Mr Bogg went home a happy man.

The evening paper which he had read, reached Scotland later that Friday night, and was being sold in the streets of Glasgow, at about half-past eight, when Fred and William were just going into a café for an evening meal.

'Let's have a look at the sport, William,' said Fred.

William turned to the back page, without even glancing at the head-lines, and the two men sat down, and put the paper between them, so that they could study the football results.

'I'll have sausages and chips, Miss,' said William to the waitress.

'Same for me,' said Fred, 'and a pot of tea. Make it strong.'

The two men ate their way silently through the meal. When they had finished, William pushed the paper into his pocket, and they strolled off to their lodgings. When William pulled off his coat in his bedroom, the newspaper fell on the floor, and the head-lines caught his eye.

William stooped down and picked up the paper. He read it slowly and then he read it again, and then he gave a shout, and was out of the room and running down the passage.

'Fred! Fred!' he shouted, flinging open Fred's door.

'Shut up, you'll wake the whole house,' mumbled Fred, who was lying in bed with nothing showing above the sheet but a tuft of hair on the top of his head.

'What's the matter, anyway? I'm asleep.'

'It's the dragon!' cried William.

'What about him?'

'He's vanished.'

'Go on,' said Fred. 'How d'you know? Oh, go away, and lemme get some sleep.'

But William pulled the bedclothes away from Fred's ears and thumped him till he was properly awake.

'It's in the paper,' he said, thrusting the crumpled pages in front of Fred's eyes. 'Look!'

DRAGON VANISHES FROM ST AUBYNS!
POLICE CALLED IN

Fred sat up, suddenly wide awake.

''Ere, what's all this?' he demanded, and started to read.

'We got to get back,' said William hoarsely. 'We got to get back to St Aubyns quick. It's them Potterfield men. They got him. I knew they was up to no good. I knew it all along. I didn't like the look of them.'

Fred thought a moment.

'We ought to get the police first. Let's phone 'em.'

'Right!' said William. 'I'll do that straight away.' He went downstairs and found a public telephone-box.

'I want the police,' he said.

In a few seconds he was through. His opening remark seemed to puzzle the Glasgow sergeant.

'There's been a dragon stolen,' said William breathlessly.

'Eh?' came an astonished voice at the other end of the line.

'It's about this dragon,' began William again.

'Noo, ye can just put yer receiver doon and go hame to bed,' said the Glasgow policeman's voice, severely. 'I'll no hae me leg pu'd.'

'I'm not pulling your leg,' said William, but the policeman had rung off.

Fred was standing at the bottom of the staircase.

'Here, let me try,' he said. 'You don't know how to talk to them.'

He rang again. After a few minutes a voice said, shortly: 'Weel?'

'I wish to give information which may help to recover some stolen property,' said Fred importantly.

'Weel?'

'I've read in the newspaper that a dragon has been stolen from St Aubyns and –'

'Noo, listen tae me,' said the policeman. 'I'm not having any nonsense aboot a dragon –'

'But it's in the newspapers,' cried Fred.

'Ye don't need to believe all ye read in the noospapers.'

'Yes, but –' began Fred, 'the London police have been called in.'

'Och, mon! The London police! This is Glasgow. We don't have dragons here, nor bees in our bonnets, neither. Noo, gae back tae bed and tae sleep.'

And he rang off.

'We'd better try Scotland Yard,' said William, despondently.

Fred lifted the receiver again.

'I want Whitehall 1212,' he said.

He was soon put through to Scotland Yard.

'This is Van-driver Number Sixteen, All England Furniture Removals Company,' he began. 'I've got information regarding the St Aubyns dragon. You take this down. Me and my mate was engaged to take the dragon to an address in Potterfield earlier this week. What? Wednesday, it was. Wednesday September 7th. Yes, we was hired – by two men. No, they didn't give their names, and we don't know 'em. Oh, yes, we was paid cash down. The address was Hickson's Barn, Broom Lane, Potterfield. Don't ring off. I want to know something. I'm fond of this dragon, I am. What? No, never you mind why I'm fond of him. It'd take too long to explain. I want to know if you'll send the flying squad out there right away.'

There was a long pause, then William said, 'Oh,' in a very disappointed voice, and put the receiver down.

'They don't believe me,' he said. 'They think I'm pulling their legs, too.'

'William,' said Fred. 'There's only one thing for it. We must go back.'

'Fred,' said William. 'We must.'

Half an hour later, the two men were at the depot, filling up the van with petrol. The night was a clear, starry one. As they drove out of Glasgow, the roads were almost empty. Through silent, sleeping towns they travelled, never slackening their pace. The empty van rattled and banged, rocked a little as they rushed round corners, bounced as they went over bumps in the road, groaned and squeaked as they pulled up at traffic lights.

They saw the dawn breaking as they drove into Doncaster, with still a hundred and fifty miles, at least five hours driving, to go. And now it was more difficult to drive fast, for the towns were waking up, and there was traffic on the roads.

In Potterfield, too, someone had woken very early, and that was Mr Bogg. He, too, saw the dawn breaking. It was four-thirty. He dressed rapidly and slipped out of the house. He walked rapidly to the outskirts of Potterfield, for now was the time he had decided to get the dragon into the travelling cage. He hoped that the creature would be sleepy,

and easy to manage, after eating the sausage rolls that he
had stuffed with sleeping pills the night before. As he
walked up to the shed, he was astonished to hear a loud
voice inside cry: 'Here he comes!' and at once there was a
roar and puffs of green smoke came billowing out of the
cracks in the plank walls. Mr Bogg stood rooted to the spot.

'What's happened?' he muttered. 'What's happened?'

Before he could utter another word, a cloud of green
smoke shot out of a small hole in the roof, and wreathed
itself into letters till the astonished Mr Bogg could read,
written in green smoke across the sky:

There was then a loud, trampling noise from inside the
barn, as though an army were marching up and down, and
the sound of two voices singing *The British Grenadiers*.

Mr Bogg summoned up his courage.

'Now, look here,' he said. 'There's no need to turn nasty
just because them sausage rolls didn't agree with you.'

His remarks were interrupted by peals of laughter from
inside the barn. Then the voice of Mr Snarkins said:

'Sausage rolls? Just use your eyes, Bogg.'

Mr Bogg looked wildly round him as though he expected to find the sausage rolls growing from a tree.

'Try looking down,' suggested Mr Snarkins, helpfully.

Mr Bogg looked down. He stooped. Lying against the wall of the barn was a large, grey rat. For a moment, Mr Bogg thought it was dead, but, on looking closer, he saw that it was fast asleep lying on its back, its paws curled up, its mouth open. Mr Bogg could even hear it gently snoring. Beside it was a grubby piece of paper with a stone on it. With trembling hands, Mr Bogg picked it up. Inside the barn there was dead silence. This is what Mr Bogg read:

We gave the sausage rolls to the rat because it said it couldn't sleep in this barn – we were making too much noise. Ha! ha!　　　　　*R. Dragon and L. Snarkins.*

Mr Bogg clenched his fist.

'That Snarkins!' he said. 'I never did trust him. Wait till I lay my hands on him.'

But before he could do another thing, there was a truly terrible sound from inside the barn. The walls shook with roars that echoed round the field, and out of every crack and slit in the planks came green smoke, till the barn was wreathed in it and looked as if it was on green fire.

Mr Boggs could stand no more. With a howl of terror, he turned and ran from the field as fast as his legs could carry him.

12

The Pageant

I⊤ was now the morning of the pageant. Up in the field stood a group of people talking sadly about the dragon's disappearance.

'I'm beginning to wonder if I didn't dream the whole thing,' the Mayor was saying. 'Was there ever a dragon at all?'

'Of course there was a dragon,' said Mrs Wotherspoon. 'I shall never forget the way he kissed my hand and said *Noblesse Oblige.*'

Mrs Wotherspoon sniffed and took out her handkerchief. The Mayor groaned. The children were sitting on the grass nearby, listening to the grown-ups.

'I think he'll come back,' said Natasha, suddenly. 'I don't believe he's the sort of dragon that would just go off and leave us, when we are all depending on him. And if something horrid has happened to him, then I think he'll get out of it by his magic.'

'The trouble is,' said Sue sadly, 'that he can't look after himself very well. You see, he left his teeth on the island. I saw them there when we looked, only I didn't say anything. He can't bite anyone now.'

'But there's his magic,' repeated Natasha.

'Well, yes,' said Sue, 'but he doesn't do much magic these days. He's out of practice.'

'It's no use just sitting and doing nothing,' said Mrs Wotherspoon, briskly. 'Now I suggest we all spend a busy morning and that will stop us thinking sad thoughts. You, Mr Mayor, get some posters out at the entrance to the field, explaining what's happened, and warning people that the first scene may have to be cut.'

'It *will* have to be, obviously,' said the Mayor, in deep gloom.

'Nonsense!' retorted Mrs Wotherspoon. 'There's no *will* about it. You won't know for certain till twenty-nine and a half minutes past two (the pageant, you remember, was due to start at two-thirty). Up till the last 30 seconds, there will still be a chance that that dragon of ours will come galloping across the field, or perhaps flying through the air. He can fly, can't he?' She turned to Susan.

'Oh, yes,' said Susan. 'He can, only he gets rather tired now.'

'Now you go and see to the posters,' said Mrs Wotherspoon, turning back to the Mayor, 'and that'll keep you occupied for the morning. Now, what about you children?'

Mrs Wotherspoon looked at them thoughtfully.

'Susan, you can come with me. Natasha, you and the boys did enough searching yesterday. You had much better have something to amuse you and take your minds off the dragon. Here's twenty-five pence. Take the bus into Barford and go to the swimming baths there.'

'We can go to the swimming baths here,' objected Natasha, 'and they're much nearer.'

'They are much better ones, deeper and longer, in Barford,' said Mrs Wotherspoon firmly, 'and it'll take you most of the morning to get there and back, which will be a very good thing.'

'I don't want to go,' said Jeremy, stubbornly. 'I don't like swimming, anyway.'

'You can watch Natasha and Richard, then,' said Mrs Wotherspoon.

'No,' said Jeremy. 'I want to stay here in the field and think. Sometimes ideas come to me.'

'All right, Jeremy,' said Mrs Wotherspoon, unexpectedly, and then, still more surprisingly, she added: 'you have some of the twenty-five pence for ice-creams, to help you think.' And she handed Jeremy five pence and gave the other two children twenty.

'Go along,' she said.

'I hate going,' said Natasha, 'but honestly it seems more sensible. There's nothing we can do by staying here.'

'Except get in people's way,' said Richard bitterly, as two men pushed him aside, and dumped a large wooden crate where he had been standing.

So Richard and Natasha went off. Jeremy sat down on the wooden crate and stared into space, and Sue turned to Mrs Wotherspoon.

'What about me?' she asked, rather forlornly.

'Well,' said Mrs Wotherspoon, taking her hand, 'I want

you to come with me in the car, and I'm going to drive all round the countryside, looking in every shed and barn we come to. Dragons can't just disappear. I think he's been hidden somewhere, and I think we shall both feel better if we go on looking for him, even if we don't find him. And as we go, you tell me everything you can about him, what he likes and what he doesn't like, and how he lives in Cornwall, and perhaps that'll help us to find out where to look.'

'He's very fond of Wales,' said Sue, suddenly. 'He can speak Welsh. I suppose he can't have flown off to Wales?'

'Oh, goodness!' said Mrs Wotherspoon. 'Wales is two hundred miles away. I can't go there and back in a morning. No, we'll have to look nearer than that.'

'And he loves the sea, too,' went on Susan.

'That's no good,' answered Mrs Wotherspoon. 'The nearest sea is over two hundred miles away. No, Sue, we'll just drive and talk. I'll do the driving and you do the talking, and that'll keep both of us occupied.'

The morning passed slowly by. Men were busy in the field, putting up last minute bits of scenery, extra benches and bunting. Jeremy was shifted from his wooden crate to a bench, and from a bench to the ground. He ate three icecreams and went on thinking. At one o'clock, just as he was leaving the field, to go home to lunch, two men got out of a furniture van at the gate and came towards him. They were Fred and William.

'Hi, young 'un!' cried Fred. 'Is there any news of this dragon?'

'News?' repeated Jeremy. 'No, only that he's lost.'

'He's not turned up yet?'

Jeremy shook his head. Fred turned to William.

'Come on,' he said. 'It's those two men, there ain't a doubt of it.'

Suddenly Jeremy remembered. He ran after the vanmen. 'Was it a fat one and a thin one?' he asked.

'It was,' answered Fred. 'Know them?'

'Not exactly, but I know what they looked like. They were always snooping about.'

'Were they?' said Fred, grimly. 'Come on, William. We'll go to the police and make 'em come out to Potterfield and find them two ruffians.'

It was a sunny day and crowds were gathering at St Aubyns to see the pageant. But crowds were gathering at Potterfield, too, to see the Visitor from Mars. When the police car arrived, it couldn't get near the lane leading to the show field, there was so much traffic and so many people jostling along it. Fred and William and the two St Aubyns policemen who had come with them, forced their way through the crowds to the gate. If it had not been for the two policemen they would never have got through, but one of them was a sergeant, and kept saying in stern tones:

'Now then, make way, please make way! This is the police.'

The two men in the ticket office looked pale and anxious.

'We daren't sell a ticket, Constable,' they said. 'The crowds are getting worse and worse, and they're angry now, but we dursn't let them into the field.'

'Why not?' demanded the policemen.

'Because – because there *ain't* no Visitor from Mars,' said one of the ticket men.

'And there ain't no Mr Bogg, neither,' said the other.

'Ho!' said the policeman. 'Ho! So he's made off, has he? Very suspicious. Sounds to me as if there never was no Visitor from Mars.'

'Yes, there was,' said Fred. 'I see it all now. It was going to be the dragon. And if we find this Mr Bogg, I bet he will be one of those unpleasant fellows who paid us to bring the dragon over here in our van.'

The two policemen turned on the ticket men.

'What's Bogg's address?' they asked.

'Number seven, Mud Street,' was the reply.

The policemen elbowed their way through the crowds again, got back in the car and started to move slowly down the lane to Potterfield. It took a long time, and they arrived at Mr Bogg's house very hot, tired and cross.

They knocked on the door and a frightened Mrs Bogg opened it. She was wearing bedroom slippers and her hair was coming down over her left ear. She looked very upset.

'Where's Mr Bogg?' asked the sergeant.

'He's – he's – not at home,' faltered the unhappy Mrs Bogg, and bursting into tears, she called over her shoulder:

'Oh, 'Enery, what 'ave you done? Here's the police!'

'He *is* at home, then?' demanded the sergeant, fiercely.

'He said I was to say he wasn't,' wept Mrs Bogg, 'but I didn't know it would be the police, indeed I didn't.'

The two policemen went into the house and in a few moments came out of the front door with a very crestfallen Mr Bogg between them.

'Is this him?' they asked.

'That's him!' cried Fred and William together.

'Right!' said the sergeant. 'You're coming back with us to St Aubyns police station to give an explanation of all this, Mr Bogg. And if anything's happened to our dragon, you'll be held responsible,' went on the sergeant in awful tones. 'I don't know what law we can say you've broken – cruelty to animals, manslaughter, unlawful detention, robbery with violence – there's no special law about dragons, as far as I know, but never mind, we'll find something.'

The two policemen, with Mr Bogg between them, and

Fred and William close behind, crowded into the police car, and set off for St Aubyns. It was now exactly two o'clock.

William and Fred whispered together for a few minutes, and then Fred turned to the sergeant.

'There's something we seem to have forgotten,' he said, 'the dragon himself. Mr Bogg ought to be able to tell us where he is, and we could go and find him, and see to this – this criminal afterwards,' and Fred glared at Mr Bogg, who said hastily :

'He was in a shed.'

'Where?'

'Just along here. Down the next turning on the left, in fact.'

The police car swung round to the left and lurched down the rough lane.

'He'll never let you get near the shed,' went on Mr Bogg, sulkily. 'That was the whole trouble. He turned nasty.'

'I don't wonder,' said William. 'I'd turn nasty if you locked me up in a shed.'

'But I was going to set him free,' pleaded Mr Bogg. 'Truly I was.'

'I don't suppose he believed you,' said William grimly. 'There's the shed.'

Crying out, 'Dragon, dragon, here we are!' the men rushed across the field.

In a moment, they had opened the doors, and the dragon was out, blinking in the sunshine, shaking hands all round, puffing and snorting and thumping his tail.

'And this is my good friend, Mr Snarkins,' he said, introducing that gentleman.

'Pleased·to meet you,' said Fred, 'though I seem to have met you before.'

'Don't mention it,' said Mr Snarkins hastily, 'I'm a changed man now.'

'Snarkins!' shouted Mr Bogg, putting his head out of the window of the police car. 'I thought the dragon had eaten you.'

'No, Mr Bogg,' called the dragon. 'I'm saving up for *you*.'

Mr Bogg withdrew his head hastily.

'Now,' said Fred, 'it's after two o'clock. In fact – goodness! – it's quarter past. How are we going to get you back to the pageant in time?'

'I might be able to fly,' said the dragon, after a moment's hesitation.

'What about your friend Snarkins? I don't think there would be room for him in the car.'

'That's all right,' said Mr Snarkins. 'I'll walk.'

'Not at all,' said the dragon. 'I shall take you with me. Now just leave us alone. I don't want a crowd around while I start. The magic mightn't work. You go and get that Bogg into prison before he gives you the slip.'

So William and Fred hurried back to the police car and never even looked over their shoulders.

The Mayor's posters were up at the entrance to the field when they arrived, warning people that the dragon might not be taking part.

'We'll drop you out here,' said the sergeant to William and Fred, 'and go on to the police station.'

So the vanmen got out and entered the pageant field. Susan and Mrs Wotherspoon had been there for some time and so had the others. Natasha had had to dress for her part just in case the dragon did come back, but now she was standing forlornly with her friends. It was twenty past two, and nobody thought he would come. Susan was silent. She and Mrs Wotherspoon had searched all morning without success. Down in her throat she could feel a large lump, and she knew that as soon as she could get away from the others, she would cry, but now she swallowed it hard and clung to Mrs Wotherspoon's hand.

The crowds were seated on benches, waiting for the pageant to begin and there was a hubbub of conversation. Snatches of it reached the children.

'Of course, I always said there wasn't no dragon.'

'Terribly disappointing all the same.'

'Where did he come from, I'd like to know?'

'You can't always believe what children say, can you? I expect they'd been to the zoo and seen a crocodile or something.'

'They don't know,' thought Sue, miserably. 'They just don't know. They don't understand about R. Dragon.'

She had spoken the last sentence out loud, though she didn't mean to, but only Jeremy, who was next to her had heard it. He looked curiously at her, and then his face suddenly changed. It got rather red, and he pulled at Susan's sleeve and whispered:

'Sue, I must speak to you. Quick, it's urgent.'

She followed him as he hurried to get out of earshot of the grown-ups.

'I've had an idea,' said Jeremy. *Call his name.*'

'His name? What d'you mean?' repeated Sue, stupidly.

'You remember. You told us you knew what the R. stood for but you had promised never never to use it except when it was urgent.'

'Yes,' said Sue, 'but I think he only meant when I was in danger, like being eaten by a wolf or something awful. I promised never to call his name for something that didn't really matter.'

'But this does really matter,' cried Jeremy. 'Oh, go on,

Sue, do try it. After all, it can't do any harm. He needn't come if he doesn't want to, and if he *is* tied up in prison or fallen down a well or something, then calling his name might somehow — I don't know how — give him magic powers to get free.'

'All right,' whispered Sue, 'I will, only you must go away, Jeremy, and put your hands over your ears and promise you won't listen.'

'All right,' said Jeremy. 'You're safe here. No one's listening, and anyway there's such a row going on no one could possibly hear you.'

Sue looked up at the blue sky, and away from the backs and shoulders and heads of people that seemed to be all round her. She took a deep breath and then, as loudly as she dared, she called the dragon by his first name. I can't tell you what it was, in case you ever called it, too, and he wouldn't want that. I can only tell you that Sue called it three times, because three is a magic number, and then she called it seven times, because seven is also a magic number, and then she said, in her natural voice:

'Do, *do* come home. I'm not in any danger, but I want you back, dear Dragon, I want you back.'

In the field near the shed, the dragon was still standing, rather sadly, with Mr Snarkins on his back.

'I'm sorry,' he said. 'I've tried the magic three times, and it just won't work. I'm out of practice, that's the trouble.'

'Perhaps I'm too heavy,' suggested Mr Snarkins, apologetically, and climbed off the dragon's back. 'You go without me, Sir Dragon.'

'I'm for the Pageant!' cried the dragon for the fourth time, even louder than before.

He spread his wings, and rose in the air a little, only to land again a few feet away.

'We'd better walk,' the dragon said, hopelessly.

'It's after half-past two,' said Mr Snarkins. 'We can't get there in time, now.'

At that very moment, Susan's voice, calling out his name, reached the dragon's ears. Mr Snarkins saw him stiffen, the yellow fins down his back suddenly shone more brightly, and he blew a powerful puff of green smoke from his nose.

'Mr Snarkins, get on my back! Quick!' ordered the dragon, and almost before Mr Snarkins had scrambled up, the dragon was shouting loudly and firmly:

'I'm for the Pageant!' and with a rush of wind in his ears, Mr Snarkins felt himself being carried up into the air.

In the pageant field itself, Sue screwed her handkerchief into a ball, and turning to Jeremy, said:

'Oh, Jeremy, I do hope he heard me.'

As she said the words, she realized that they sounded very loud indeed, and this was because all the hubbub of voices had suddenly ceased. No one was speaking in all that vast crowd. They were all looking upwards, and craning their necks. And then, at last, a great shout went up:

'There he is!'

Sue jumped onto the end of a bench, and there was the dragon, R. Dragon himself, sailing through the sky with his great wings outspread. He circled lower and lower over the pageant field, and then Sue could see that there was someone on his back. It was Mr Snarkins. The dragon made a perfect landing on the grassy plateau that formed the stage, and Mr Snarkins climbed off his back. A gasp of astonishment went up from the spectators. The dragon quickly held up a green paw.

'Silence, please!' he cried. 'We're only just in time for the pageant. Pageant first, explanations afterwards.'

With which he hurried off behind the scenes, leaving a bewildered Mr Snarkins on the stage.

'It's one of the Potterfield men,' cried Jeremy. 'Call the police!'

At this there was pandemonium. There were shouts of 'Police! Police!' 'Stop Thief!' and so on, while some people, not knowing quite what was happening, shouted: 'Send for a doctor!' and 'Help! Help!' and even 'Fire! Fire!'

Mr Snarkins was looking very frightened.

'Go on, Mr Mayor,' urged Mrs Wotherspoon. 'You'll have to say something. The crowd's going mad.'

'I don't know what to say,' said the Mayor, waving his hands helplessly.

'Then I'll say it,' cried Mrs Wotherspoon, and marched onto the platform, with her artificial flowers waving like banners.

'Ladies and Gentlemen,' she cried. 'We all want to know what has happened to our dragon who has been miraculously restored to us at the last moment. Here he is to tell you himself.'

There was a deafening roar of applause and cheering, whistles and shrieks as the dragon stepped onto the stage, bowing to right and left, and breathing out puffs of green smoke from his nostrils. The Mayor shook him warmly by the paw and the dragon turned to the audience.

'Mr Mayor, Ladies and Gentlemen,' he began. 'I have had an exciting three days. Not since those far-distant times of King Arthur, when dragons and giants, I may tell you, were as common as caterpillars, do I remember having such an exciting three days. First I was captured –'

A groan went up from the crowd.

'– captured by two men from Potterfield.'

The crowd hissed and booed.

'Down with Potterfield!' shouted someone, but the dragon held up his paw, and the crowd fell silent again.

'I was locked in a barn,' he went on, 'a smelly, dark barn, by two gentlemen called Snogg and Barkins.'

'No, no!' came an agonized voice from the side of the stage. 'No, no, yer honour, Bogg and Snarkins.'

'Ah, yes,' said the dragon, correcting himself. 'Bogg and Snarkins. One of them, however, Mr Snarkins, was, by an accident, locked into the barn with me. I could, of course, have eaten him' (the dragon here licked his lips thoughtfully, and a voice from the crowd called 'Why didn't you?').

The dragon then coughed behind his paw and went on: 'It was not very convenient. I suppose I could have used magic to turn him into a toad or – or a centipede or something unpleasant like that.'

'You should have done!' called a voice from the crowd. 'Serve him right! Down with Snarkins!'

'No, no,' said the Dragon. 'Don't say, "Down with Snarkins" yet. I had a better idea. I decided to turn him into a new Mr Snarkins, a pleasant, honest, respectable Mr Snarkins. I talked to him, I persuaded him, and in no time, he came round to my side.'

'Hooray!' shouted the crowd, delighted at the dragon's success with Mr Snarkins.

'As for how I escaped from the barn, that was entirely due to the efforts of my good friends Fred and William, whom I think I see' – and the dragon reached out his long neck and peered from right to left among the crowd – 'yes – there they are! – sitting among you.'

All heads turned in one direction, and there sat William and Fred blushing as red as beetroots.

A clock struck three.

'Goodness!' cried the dragon. 'I've been making a very long speech. Pray forgive me.' And he hurried off the platform to loud applause.

The pageant now started properly. The ancient Britons strutted onto the stage and one of them began his speech:

'Britons! Attend and mark! For many years our land has been ravaged by a terrible dragon; our children eaten; our herds of cattle stolen, our villages terrorized. This dragon is our deadliest enemy.'

The crowd of Britons groaned and wept and waved their arms with grief.

'Our fair and goodly fields are laid waste!' they cried. 'What shall we do?'

Into their midst strode a tall figure, clad in a long white garment, rather like a nightdress. It was Mr Barker, the man who played St Aubyn, and owned the collie dog, Bing.

'What is the matter?' he cried. 'What is all this weeping and wailing?'

Before the ancient Britons could answer him, onto the stage trotted Bing.

There was loud applause and laughter. St Aubyn looked down at Bing, angrily.

'You bad dog!' he whispered. 'Go home! Go home! Home!'

But Bing only wagged his tail furiously and whimpered with excitement.

'I'll take him,' shouted Jeremy, and rushed onto the stage. He caught Bing by the collar and dragged him off.

The pageant then got going again.

'What is the matter?' cried St Aubyn. 'What is all this weeping and wailing?'

'It is the dragon,' answered the Britons. 'He eats our flocks, he murders our families. He –'

And at that moment, there was a dreadful roaring, and, amid clouds of green smoke, the dragon rushed onto the stage holding Natasha in his jaws. A gasp went up from the audience. It looked very terrible. One woman near Sue uttered a shriek and nearly fainted.

'It's all right,' said Sue hastily. 'He hasn't any teeth.'

But by this time, the woman had fainted right off and had to be carried from the field. The Britons scattered. Only St Aubyn stood firmly in the centre of the stage. The dragon eyed him furiously, lashing his tail and growling.

'Dragon, I do not fear you,' cried St Aubyn, drawing his sword.

The dragon growled more loudly and rolled his eyes.

'I command you, lay down that child and do battle with me.'

The dragon shook his head (really quite gently, because of Natasha being in his mouth).

'Lay her down!' commanded the saint, advancing with his sword. 'Lay her down or I will run you through the heart.'

The dragon backed away for a moment, and then, dropping Natasha (very carefully so that he did not hurt her), he did a few dancing steps with his feet, and rushed towards St Aubyn.

There was a fearful battle.

The dragon sent out such clouds of smoke that it was quite difficult to see what was going on. At one moment he had St Aubyn lying flat on the ground and placed a great scaly paw upon his chest, but St Aubyn prodded him with his sword and the dragon jumped away. At last, with a cry of 'Death to the Dragon!' St Aubyn lunged forward, and thrust his sword into the dragon's heart. Of course, he didn't really do this. He slipped his sword behind the dragon's shoulder, but from the front it looked exactly as if the blade had gone right in. With a fearful howl, the dragon lay down, rolled over and lashed his tail. His lashings grew feebler and feebler, and at last with a sigh he turned over on his back with his legs in the air and his eyes tight shut, pretending to be dead. St Aubyn placed a foot upon his stomach, and waved his sword and cried:

'The dragon is dead!'

The audience became very excited. They shouted and clapped, and the dragon at once got up to show he wasn't really dead, and walked to the front of the stage, hand in paw with St Aubyn and Natasha. All three stood bowing and smiling. Then they went off and the next scene of the pageant started.

The children simply couldn't bear to sit through it. They

had to go behind the scenes and see the dragon. And so did Mrs Wotherspoon. They found the dragon sitting on an upturned wooden box, with Natasha beside him, and Mr Snarkins opposite. All three were drinking lemonade through straws, only the dragon's lemonade was in a large bottle, while the other two had ordinary tumblers.

'Acting makes one thirsty,' he observed. 'My word, that was a fight!'

'You were wonderful,' cried the children. 'You really looked as if you were going to eat Natasha at any moment.'

'I saw it all from the wings,' said Mr Snarkins. 'I said to myself, that dragon's as good as any film star I've ever seen.'

The dragon looked very pleased.

'Allow me to introduce Mr Snarkins,' he said. 'Mrs Wotherspoon, this is my friend Mr Snarkins. Susan, Richard, Jeremy – Mr Snarkins.'

'You're the man from Potterfield,' said Susan, accusingly, still feeling very distrustful.

'Well, yes,' answered Mr Snarkins, blushing, 'but I'm a changed man from now on.'

'Even his name,' interposed the dragon, 'isn't really Snarkins. I've discovered he's actually Welsh – Llewellyn Ap Snarkins, that's his real name. Not that he speaks any Welsh, poor man. I've taught him one or two things, "Bore da" for instance, which means "Good morning", and "Lawr i Bogg", which means "Down with Bogg".'

'*Lawr i Bogg!*' repeated Mr Snarkins, with deep feeling. 'Oh, how I wish I'd never got mixed up with Bogg.'

'Well, you're unmixed now,' said Susan, comfortingly. 'Mr Bogg's in prison.'

'Which is the best place for him,' cried William and Fred, who had now joined the party.

'Have we any more lemonade for William and Fred?' asked the dragon.

'Not a drop,' answered Mr Snarkins.

'I suggest the children go and buy some more,' said Mrs Wotherspoon and opened her large, plum-coloured handbag. She gave Richard a fifty-pence piece.

'I say,' he exclaimed. 'Fifty pence! It'll buy pints.'

'We need pints,' said William in a gloomy voice, 'We've had nothing to eat or drink since about nine o'clock last night.'

The whole party looked in amazement at the noble William and Fred.

'We'd no time,' explained Fred, modestly. 'We felt that the important thing was to get down here and rescue the dragon.'

Mrs Wotherspoon opened her plum-coloured bag once more.

'Richard,' she said. 'Here is another twenty-five pence. You must buy some sandwiches for these gentlemen.'

'Oh, no, mum,' said William, hastily. 'Oh, no, really.'

'Nonsense,' said Mrs Wotherspoon, firmly. 'I am partly responsible for this pageant, and we couldn't have done it without you, so of course we must provide you with sandwiches.'

The four children rushed off to buy the food and drink, and eventually returned with a huge bag of sandwiches for Fred and William, a bag of doughnuts for everyone else, two bottles of ginger beer (the children thought that ginger beer would suit Fred and William better than lemonade) and a dozen bottles of assorted fruit drinks, raspberry, lemon, orange and cherry.

'And,' said Richard, 'we've got a cup of tea for you, Mrs Wotherspoon. It was Sue's idea,' he added.

Sue stepped forward and offered Mrs Wotherspoon a cup of rather dark brown tea.

'I'm afraid most of it's slopped into the saucer,' she said, apologetically.

'Never mind,' said Mrs Wotherspoon. 'It was a very kind thought.'

Meanwhile, the pageant was drawing to a close, and by the time they had finished all the food and drink, the last act was beginning. They all went out and watched this, and at the end, the whole cast came onto the stage, among them, of course, the dragon and Natasha.

'What about your Visitor from Mars, eh?' demanded William, turning to Mr Snarkins.

'Don't remind me of that,' groaned Mr Snarkins. 'It was a wicked idea. But, I keep telling you, I'm a changed man. I won't never do things like that no more.'

When at last the clapping and cheering died away, and the crowds began to break up, the dragon and Natasha returned to the group, and everyone felt rather flat.

'What shall we do now?' asked the children. 'The fireworks don't begin for at least three hours.'

The dragon looked round them.

'Well,' he said, 'I, for one, am going to have a rest before the fireworks. But before I go off to my little island, I am going to tell you all an important decision that I've come to. I'm going back to Cornwall. I've enjoyed this pageant very much, but, well, the week has been an exciting one, and a bit too much for a dragon of my advanced years. I need quiet, solitude, the sea, my midnight bathes under the stars, my own cosy cave to sleep in. I think this is the moment to say goodbye to you all.'

'But I've only just met you,' wailed Mr Snarkins.

'Next year,' said the dragon, firmly shaking his hand, 'you must spend your summer holiday in Cornwall and come and see me. Constantine Bay. That'll find me. Goodbye, Mr Snarkins, Da boch! as we say in Welsh. Fred and William, I'm sure we shall be meeting again. I expect you come to Cornwall sometimes in your van?'

'Of course we do,' they cried, 'and we'll be sure to come and see you.'

'We'll sing *Daisy, Daisy,* by the seashore,' said William.

'It will sound lovely,' agreed the dragon.

'And play chess on the rocks,' added Fred.

'I'll look forward to that,' answered the dragon, and shook paws with them both.

He then turned to Mrs Wotherspoon, and took her hand.

'Farewell, Lady Wotherspoon,' he said in his grandest manner. 'I shall never forget you.'

'Or her hat,' whispered Sue in Jeremy's ear.

The dragon turned round.

'I heard you,' he said sternly, and kissed Mrs Wotherspoon's hand most gallantly.

He said 'Da boch!' both to Richard and Jeremy, and then to Natasha, giving them all a warm invitation to visit him at Constantine Bay, and finally he turned to Sue.

'I wondered if you would like to come to the island with me,' he said.

'Oh, I would,' cried Susan. So they went off together, and the others broke up and went their different ways, the children first arranging to meet in the evening, to see the firework display.

13

I'm for Constantine Bay

THE dragon and Susan walked silently down to the lake. There seemed to be nothing much either of them wanted to say. Susan had known, of course, that the dragon would not want to stay in St Aubyns always, but even if you know something is going to happen, you do not feel it properly until it does happen. When they got to the lake, the dragon, as if he had known exactly what Sue was thinking, suddenly said:

'Of course, I could always come here again on a visit now I know what the place is like, and have got an island to come to. I expect William and Fred would bring me up here on their way back from Cornwall some time.'

'Oh, yes, that would be lovely,' cried Susan, feeling much

brighter. 'We could keep your island clean and tidy for you, couldn't we, so that it is always ready, like a sort of spare room?'

'That's a very pleasing idea,' said the dragon. 'Now climb onto my back and I'll swim across. Keep your feet well up or they'll get wet.'

Susan climbed up on the scaly, bony back, and as she clutched it, she remembered how she had sat there the year before when the dragon had flown through the sky with her, and how exciting it had been to look down on Tintagel Castle and see the people round it, like ants round a grey tree stump.

'Dear Dragon,' she said, absently, stroking his scales.

They were across the lake very quickly. The dragon climbed out and when Susan had got down, he shook the water off himself, and looked round at his belongings.

'How are you going to get all this back?' asked Susan.

'That's just it,' answered the dragon. 'I'm not sure. I was thinking of flying back in easy stages, taking a few days over it. But I can't carry all this. I suppose I could manage *some* of it.'

'Well,' said Sue, 'if you're going to make this your spare room, couldn't you leave some of it? Perhaps Daddy would keep it in the garage for you, so it wouldn't get wet and spoilt.'

The dragon was very pleased with this idea.

'I think I'll leave the sewing machine lid,' he said, 'and the mouse-trap.'

'Couldn't you leave some blankets?' suggested Sue. 'After all, you've got quite a lot in your cave.'

After some hesitation, the dragon decided he could spare two out of the three, and he and Susan folded them up very carefully, and put them with the lid and the mouse-trap.

They made two piles, and then the dragon tied up the things he was going to take, like his teeth and his one blanket, and his washing things, and his long green scarf, and his handkerchiefs with R.D. embroidered in the corner.

'I think I could carry *them* on my back,' he said, 'if you'll look after the rest.'

'I'll get the boys to come over here in a boat,' said Susan, 'and we'll take them back to our house.'

'Now,' said the dragon, 'we're both tired. I am specially tired because I have been acting in a pageant, and you are ordinarily tired.'

'I think I'm specially tired, too,' said Susan, 'because I've been searching for a dragon all day.' She felt a little indignant.

'Well, yes,' answered the dragon, kindly. 'Perhaps you are. Anyway, I think we both need a rest before the fireworks. I am going to sleep.'

'When – when are you actually going?' asked Sue.

The dragon said nothing for a moment, then he answered:

'I think it would be best if I set off after the firework display. I like travelling by night. I can guide myself by the stars.'

'It seems dreadfully soon,' faltered Sue.

'You'll find,' said the dragon, 'that once you've made up your mind to leave somewhere, it's much best to get going and not linger. That only makes it sadder. If I'm going, I'll go tonight.'

'I'll make you a picnic for the journey,' said Sue.

'Ah,' said the dragon, 'I said before that you would make a wonderful wife to an explorer. You think of all the right things.'

'I'll go and make it now,' said Sue, 'while you're having

a sleep, and then *I'll* have a rest and come and fetch you when we all go to the field for the fireworks.'

The dragon closed his eyes.

'That's a perfect idea,' he said.

'There's just one thing,' said Susan, 'that I wanted to ask you. You didn't mind my calling your name, did you?'

The dragon opened one eye.

'No,' he said. 'I was rather glad, as a matter of fact. You see, there's magic in names, and when I heard you calling mine, as I was trying to fly away from that horrible Potterfield, it gave me the magic power to get into the air.'

'You didn't think I was being eaten by a wolf?'

'Not exactly. I just heard my name, and I knew I must hurry because you needed me. If you had actually been in danger the name would have sounded still more urgent, and the magic would have worked so quickly that I should have reached you almost before you'd stopped calling for me.'

'Poor Mr Snarkins!' cried Sue. 'If you'd done that, he'd have fallen off.'

'He very nearly did as it was,' said the dragon.

He was just about to close his eyes again, when he suddenly remembered that Sue couldn't get back from the island. So he took her over, and when she had watched him swim back and lie down again, she walked home.

'I've got to get a picnic for the dragon,' she said, rather wearily.

'You're doing nothing of the sort,' said her mother. 'You're going to have an hour's sleep before the fireworks start. Must he have a picnic?'

'He's starting off for Cornwall tonight,' said Sue. 'I must get it ready. I promised him.'

'I'll get it, then,' said her mother. 'I'll make it a really nice one, if it's a farewell picnic. You go to bed.'

Later on that evening, Sue and her mother fetched the
dragon, and he swam across the lake with his bundle on his
back, and came with them to the firework field, where they
met the others. It was a splendid display, with dozens of
rockets going off all at the same time, and rows of catherine
wheels fastened to posts, and the showers of golden rain and
coloured fountains spraying up into the night sky so held
the children's attention that they never noticed the dragon
go. Sue suddenly saw, in the dark blue sky, among the flash
of the rockets, what looked like a bright green, moving star.
She turned round, and the dragon had gone. She clutched
Natasha's hand. 'That's the dragon,' she whispered, and
pointed to the green star which was mounting over the tree
tops, higher and higher.

'There he goes!' And she waved, hoping that the dragon
would see her white hand waving. He must have done, for
the golden shower of rockets was hidden, just for a moment,
in a cloud of green smoke, and a wisp of it came floating
down towards her waving hand – a dragon's kiss.

About the Author

Rosemary Manning was born in Dorset in 1911. After taking a Classics Degree, she has had a varied career in business, teaching, and lecturing, though she would describe her main profession as that of writer. In addition to five children's books, she has written several novels for adults and a number of short stories. She now lives for much of the year in the West Country, which she knows well and uses as the setting for many of her books, including this one, and *Green Smoke*.

Some other Puffins you might enjoy

Also by Rosemary Manning
GREEN SMOKE

The first book about Susan and the dragon, who was 1,500 years old and had a partiality for almond buns. He could also tell stories and Sue heard about the Cornish giants and fairies, and of King Arthur whom he had known very well. He taught Sue songs and took her on trips to Tintagel Castle and the Pool of Excalibur, and once to have tea with a mermaid, who told her about the country under the sea.

THE KINGDOM OF CARBONEL
Barbara Sleigh

Carbonel, King of the Cats, needed help to guard his two royal kittens while he was away, so of course he turned to his old companions John and Rosemary. They were naturally proud to be entrusted with the kittens, but it was a difficult job with such high spirited youngsters and especially with Queen Grisana aided by Mrs Cantrip ever on the watch to trap the kittens and invade Fallowhithe. But they hardly expected it to lead to adventures like John being made invisible (a hungry state, he found, as he could hardly turn up for meals when Rosemary's mother couldn't see him), or being run away with by a very dimwitted magic rocking chair and stranded all night on top of the tallest building in Fallowhithe.

THE DRIBBLESOME TEAPOTS AND OTHER
INCREDIBLE STORIES

Norman Hunter

'Oh, oh, oh, oh! This is terrible,' cried the Queen. 'Not a teapot in the Palace that can be used. Oh, disgraceful! I must have a teapot that doesn't dribble, I must! I must! Half the kingdom as a reward for anyone who can bring me a teapot that pours without dribbling!'

'Here, here, here, half a mo!' cried the King, getting all agitated. 'You can't do that. What do you think's going to happen to Sypso-Sweetleigh if you go offering half of it for teapots?' But it was too late. Before he could be stopped the Royal Herald had shouted the proclamation all round the city, and we leave you to work out how the King and Queen got out of the difficulties it caused, without breaking their royal word.

By the author of three other celebrated Puffins – *The Incredible Adventures of Professor Branestawm*, *Professor Branestawm's Treasure Hunt*, and *The Puffin Book of Magic*.

MAGIC BY THE LAKE

Edward Eager

'Have you noticed the name on the cottage?' asked Katharine. She and Jane and Mark and Martha (the children in *Half Magic*) had just arrived at their holiday cottage with their mother and their new stepfather, Mr Smith.

'Magic by the Lake,' said Martha. 'Doesn't it sound lovely? Don't you wish it were true?'

Then Mark's turtle stuck its head out of its shell. 'Now you've done it,' it said. 'You couldn't be sensible, could you, and order magic by the pound, for instance, or by the day? Or by threes, the good old-fashioned way? You had to be greedy and order magic by the lake, and of course now you've got a whole lakeful of it.'

Readers of *Half Magic* will already know Mr Eager's particular blend of enchantment, with its mixture of humour, wild adventure, and everyday happenings.